Nadine Hanley

Never Should've Loved Him

Nadine Hanley

NJS BOOKS

njsbooks16@yahoo.com

nadine.hanley16@gmail.com

Never Should've Loved Him

Never Should've Loved Him

Never Should've Loved Him

DEDICATION

This book is dedicated to all the women that has ever loved someone with all their heart, even though you knew that he could not love you back the way you wanted or needed to be loved. To those who have ever been a fool for love in your life. And to those who just love too much and too hard that a man can't understand it or accept it for what it is and what it's worth.

To my Mom Anita, and my kids, who have supported everything I have ever set out to do. And to my friends. Thank you and I love you much.

Nadine...

Nadine Hanley

ACKNOWLEDGMENTS

This book is dear to my heart for so many reasons. Because like so many women I to have loved hard, and with everything in me. I would just like to thank the man above, my Lord Jesus Christ, for all the blessings in my life. And to all the people who gave me the push to write this book and all my other books.

Thank you.
Much Love Nadine.

Never Should've Loved Him

Prologue

I felt like he was placing me under some kind of spell or hypnotizing me... The tingling sensation in Jessica's body was a feeling she had not felt in a long ass time.

"Your pussy is so damn good Jessica; I don't want to stop eating it."

That made her pussy wetter than it was.

"This pussy is so damn juicy and wet, damn, how this pussy gets so wet like this?"

He asked and all Jessica could do was moan in response. Greg began to tease her for a while, she hated when he did this.

"Why are you teasing me?" Jessica asked.

"Teasing is pleasing, and you deserve to be teased."

Chapter One

Jessica sighed and drank the rest of her drink.

"I know Lynne; it's as if I live my life the same way everyday as before. Even my weekends are boring and predictable as hell. I hope my life will not always be this damn boring... bland." Lynne looked at her sister as if she was crazy or something.

"Jessica, you're only forty-four girl, your kids are grown and on their own. If you feel like your life is so boring, do something about it. Get out and meet new people, get a new hobby or something."

Jessica shrugged. "I have done that already. I go line dancing on Wednesdays at the Fox Trot Lounge.

Sometimes I feel as if I don't fit in anywhere." Lynne picked up her check to pay on the way out.

"I don't know what to say Jessica, you've always been a loner by nature, but you've got to open yourself up more. Get out and get a new man or something." Jessica followed Lynne out of Ray's Chicken and Fish restaurant and rolled her eyes at her sister as they got into the car. Getting a new man was easy for Lynne, but not for Jessica.
In addition, a new man was not the solution to the problem at hand.

"Finding a good man isn't easy Lynne. Not for me anyway." Lynne shook her head.

"You shouldn't sell yourself short, Jessica you are a beautiful woman. You're still young, and you don't need all that makeup to look good like some women. I'm envious of you, for real." Jessica rolled her eyes and laughed.

"Girl you are not envious of me."

"Quit, Jessica you have a nice body, you've lost weight since you've been line dancing and working out. However, you are still a work in progress. It will take time to get where you want to be. Plus, Rome wasn't built in a day." Jessica hit Lynne in the arm, "fuck you Lynne, but I love you anyway. Don't know what I would do without you."

"I don't know either. Any who back to your boring life."

"Yeah, and what about it?" Lynn laughed.

"You need a vacation."

The light changed, and they drove down the street.

"I don't know, it's been a long time, some years since I had a vacation."

"Where did you go on your last vacation?"

"Disney World."

Lynne looked at her with a disgusted look on her face.

"You mean to tell me that your last vacation was years ago, and it was with Jaden at Disney World?" Jessica shrugged.

"It was a family vacation for a few weeks."

Lynne shook her head and drove on.

"Girl you need to get your sexy ass on a plane and go somewhere new. Someplace warm and tropical, someplace exciting."

"Like where?" Jessica asked. She'd always had a problem with making decisions about doing anything for herself. If left up to her, she would not go on a vacation. Lynne shrugged.

"I don't know, how about you write down six or seven places you would like to go visit. Put them in a bowl and pick one. It shouldn't matter where you go. Since your life is as boring as you say."

"That sounds like fun. When I get home, I will do just that."

Lynne rolled her eyes. "Yeah right." Jessica hated when people doubted her, even her sister.

"Okay, you'll see." Lynne dropped Jessica off at home, getting out of the car; she hugged her sister and dreading going into her lonely house.

At that moment, she decided to take a much-needed vacation, and she would take a chance on the destination by picking it out of a bowl. Jessica's dream of owning her own business was finally happening. She was weeks away from starting a new life and new business. Jessica wiped the frown off her face and thought she would show her sister she could be adventurous.

Later that night, Jessica put six pieces of paper in a bowl with the places she wanted to go on her vacation. The list of potential places was random although Jessica did a good job of picking the destinations all over the country.

Some of the places were just places on her bucket list to visit one day.
However, she planned to be true to whatever she picked. No matter what she picked, she would book her trip to start in the next three weeks. She will put in her vacation time at work the following night.

Now all that is left is to pick the destination for her vacation.

"Here we go." Jessica shook the bowl mixing up the folded pieces of paper inside. Jessica reached in three times to grab a piece of paper and each time she pulled back. Jessica felt it was not quite the right time to gamble. As she took a deep breath and closed her eyes and just grabbed a piece of paper.

"Let it be Vegas! Please let it be Vegas!"

Chapter 2

North Carolina

Jessica sighed and made a silent prayer. North Carolina was one of the last places she added to the list. She knew little about North Carolina except that Myrtle Beach and her cousin Amber were down that way.

Oh well, the city was on the list and Jessica said she would promise to honor the results. In addition, it had advantages. There was a beach, some sightseeing, tours shopping. Most of all she could spend time with her cousin Amber. She called to let her cousin know that she would be visiting in a few weeks, so that she would be looking out for her arrival.

Jessica arrived at the airport in North Carolina, June tenth at one o'clock in the afternoon. Her cousin Amber was there to meet her. They exchanged hugs and kisses on the cheek. Amber was excited that Jessica had come to visit her in N.C. and would be staying for three weeks. Even though Amber had to work, she still had plans for them to hang out. Amber took Jessica to her hotel 'The Sea Crest Oceanfront Resort' where she would stay for the next three weeks of her vacation.

"Jessica I'll pick you up later after you've had time to settled in."

"That will be cool, Amber. I'll be ready."

"You do know that you are welcome to stay with me in my guest room?" Amber told her. Jessica hugged her cousin Amber and laughed.

"I know Amber, but I didn't want to put you out or anything. Because I know you have to work and all, and this way I can get out on my own and enjoy the town some."

Jessica was relaxing by the pool at her hotel when she saw someone who looked familiar to her. Someone she has not seen in twenty years. She watched as the guy walked back into the hotel.

"No, it couldn't be, not the Greg Randall," Jessica said in a whisper. Damn the brother was still fine. She thought, Jessica started fantasizing about the time she and Greg had spent together all those years ago. And those were the best times of her life. She soon came back to reality, because he broke up with her to be with someone else, she thought to herself.

Greg was not for sure if what he saw was real or if his imagination was playing tricks on him. He could have sworn he saw Jessica sitting in one of the lounge chairs out by the pool.

It couldn't have been her he thought, not after twenty years. The love of his life just could not be staying in the same hotel as he. Greg went to his room with Jessica on his mind. Greg thought about the last time they were together how much he has really missed Jessica, and how he had searched for her, to get her back so many years ago.

He thought how he could have been so stupid to let her go, so long ago.

Greg chuckled as he made a shot of 1800 Sliver in his room. As the burn of his drink went down his throat, he closed his eyes and remembered the way Jessica smelled, felt and the way she tasted. With a smile on his face, he put down his glass, and hopped in the shower to cool down from all the tantalizing memories that flooded his mind with feelings he thought were gone for Jessica...

There was a knock-on Jessica's door.

"Who is it?" Jessica asked.

"Who else? Your cousin Amber." Jessica chuckled as she let her cousin in.

"Where are we going tonight?" Asked Jessica.

"There is a beach party tonight, down on the beach a little way down from here." Amber said.

"There will be so many people there, so dress nice and comfy, you might meet someone." She laughed, "plus they have some of the best food at these beach parties."

Jessica looked at Amber out the corner of her eyes and shook her head at her cousin. After a quick shower, Jessica slipped on an ankle-length, blue-colored spaghetti-strap dress, which had a full-buttoned down front. The body-hugging dress accentuated her curves and slim waist, and with her shoulder length curly hair pulled up off her neck, she thought she looked very sexy and attractive.

She slipped on a pair of matching sandals, and her body purse, adding some of her favorite perfume; she was ready to enjoy herself.

"You look nice, Jessica," Jessica turned around and smiled at Amber who was wearing a peach-colored cotton dress that flared out around her knees.

"Are we meeting up with some of your friends at the beach, or is it going to be us two hanging out?" Jessica asked, a smile playing at the corners of her mouth, at the anticipation of meeting new people, and feasting on some of the fantastic food and drinks. She would have to work out double time at the gym when she got back to Dayton...

"We're meeting up with Jason and his friend, who is here on vacation as well."

"What you mean Jason and his friend?"

"Well Jason has a friend from Dayton who's visiting for three weeks also, he arrived yesterday." The blood started pounding in Jessica's head.

"So, this is a blind date then?" Jessica asked.

"Not really. We are just hanging out and his friend is in town, and you are in town so we thought we would all hang out together. I'm not setting you up, Jessica. Maybe you should leave your mind and heart open to the possibilities and just let things happen naturally." Jessica looked at her cousin, Amber and shook her head.

Chapter 3

"YOU are not always going to look as good as you do, you know. At some point, you will put on weight. You're pretty hair will turn grey, and your taut impeccable skin will begin to sag and age at some point. So, play while the sun is still hot, girl. Because the sun will go down, and the crow's feet will start to appear all over your beautiful face."

Jessica laughed. It was so hard to stay mad at Amber, especially when she started using her crazy metaphors and analogies.

"So, do you know anything about this friend of Jason's?" Jessica asked, grudgingly.

"I met him about a year ago when he came out for the summer. He was here for a few days visiting friends and family. Besides the fact he's cute on the outside, he is truly a nice and terrific guy on the inside."

"How do you know he's nice? You have only spent a few days with him. You can't know somebody in such a short period."

"Well, you know Jason and like him, right? They are very much alike," she gave Jessica a sidelong glance.

Jessica's stomach began to form knots.

"How much alike are they?" Amber said something under her breath.

"What did you say?"

"He's an independent contractor, he owns his own construction business." Jessica took a deep breath to keep from getting mad.

"Look, Jessica I know you better than anyone else on this earth. There is still love in that big heart of yours that you have managed to build a wall around. You're beautiful, loving, and smart..."

"And I have asked everyone to stay out my personal life. So now add one more adjective to the list-Mad! Mad as hell! Amber you know that I said I would never date another construction guy, mainly one that travels all the time. They have secret families all over the place. I was involved with one twenty years ago and he left for another woman and a child they had together that he claimed he didn't know about."

"All construction workers are not like that guy who broke your heart a long time ago. Jason's friend is not like that."

"How do you know?"

"Because Jason trusts him, and I trust Jason. Relax, girl. It's not like you're planning to marry the guy."

"Seriously, Jessica, you need to live a little. Ever since you found out what Brandon was doing; you have given up on men. There are nice guys out there, and I know there is one with your name written on his heart. you will never know it with that attitude."

She put her hand on Jessica's arm.

"You're my cousin, my sister girl and I want you to be happy as me one day. Sooner rather than later, I hope. However, just for tonight, meet Jason's friend and try to enjoy yourself. Do it for me, please."

After a long deep silence, Jessica gave Amber a noncommittal smile,

"okay, fine, fine I will try to have a good time. And I don't care how good looking or fine this friend is; I will not let my guard down for one second."

She opened the car door and stepped out. Jessica waved at Jason who was standing on the porch with a big ass smile on his face at the sight of my cousin Amber.

With Jason's friend nowhere in sight, that was ok with Jessica, because she needed a little time to get her frazzled thoughts together and put on her, I am having-a-good-time look.

Jessica slipped off her sandals and walked to the wooden gazebo under a tree. She leaned against the railing and allowed the magnificent breeze to calm her spirits. She watched as the sun slipped behind the horizon and transformed the blue sky into a beautiful canvas of cobalt, violet and amber tones.

Never have she seen such splendor. Jessica dreamed of one day moving to a place like this, perhaps to an island somewhere, but she knew that Brandon would not let her take their son so far away. He was such a lousy two-timing, ass-whole of a husband, but he was always a good father to their son.

Jessica sighed. She had come to North Carolina to relax and get herself back together and not think about her pending divorce from Brandon. As she closed her eyes, and took a deep breath, exhaled, and let all the emotions out her mouth into the air-

"Beautiful. Just Beautiful."
Jessica's body became taut as ever, at the sound of the deep sexy masculine voice behind her. Those three words resonated throughout her body like echoing notes of a sad love song.

Jessica prayed her heart would stop beating so hard and fast. She foolishly wondered how the sound of one man's voice could affect her the way it did after all these years, especially after she had spent the last four years building a wall between her heart and the opposite sex. Maybe it was because he caught her in an emotional state, she thought.

However, when the leaves of the trees moved gently above her, and the soft genital breeze, filled with his masculine scent softly touched her nose, Jessica realized that it was not just Greg's voice that affected her; it was his familiar scent as well.

Jessica felt sedated and warm all over, all her senses remembered all too well of his presence.

"Yes, it is beautiful," She said as her voice trembled.

"I was referring to you Jessica." He whispered.

"But yes, the sunset is beautiful as well. Almost as beautiful as you Jessica."

At that moment, Jessica assumed that Jason and Amber had been talking about her and knew all along that she and Greg knew each other. Jessica turned around. Greg was a massive hunk of brown flesh. He was taller than she remembered.

He took a step towards her, bringing with him the dark heat of his sexy body dangerously closer and closer to her. Jessica's breathing became labored, and her breast swelled beneath the material of her dress, and her nipples had the nerve to get hard at the thought of what he could do to them. Jessica licked her lips as she watched Greg approach her, he was dressed in a creamed colored linen suit, with black Kenneth Cole flats.

Jessica's gaze went to the bulge of his pants. He is one blessed man; this she knew all too well. She had to force her gaze back to his chest. Jessica wanted to say something, but she could not get her tongue to come unglued from the roof of her mouth.

"Look at me Jessica." He said with such urgency in his voice. Jessica raised her head to look into his eyes. Her heart skipped a beat maybe two when their eyes connected. They were the most intense, brown magnetic eyes she had ever seen. Her body exploded deep down inside.
Jessica felt trapped at the moment, she wanted to run but her feet and legs would not allow her to.

"Hi, Jessica," he said.

"You are more beautiful than I remembered." Jessica tried to speak, but again her words had eluded her.

Her body felt heavy, yet light enough to soar into the night sky if a heavy breeze came along. Jessica's heart began beat hard against her chest, and she did not know if it was fear or excitement of seeing him again.

I have never felt this powerless, or this vulnerable in the presence of any man before except this one.

"Well, it's good to see the two of you getting along so well." Amber said and broke the spell. Jessica turned to watch her cousin and Jason coming towards them hand in hand, and both in their swimwear. Jason shrugged, "Jessica Jackson meet, Greg Randall. Jessica is Amber's cousin."

"We already know each other, we met twenty years ago." Greg said.

"Oh, okay! Well now that we have that out of the way why don't you two go change into your swimsuits?"

"I thought we were going to a beach party, and I dressed according to what you said, but I can see you lied to me Amber."

She gave Amber an I'm-going-to -kill-you look and then looked at Greg. Jessica did not like the effects he was having on her after all these years. There was just no way she was going to strip down to a skimpy bikini in front of him.

CHAPTER 4

"Forgot my swimsuit, so I guess I will have to sit this one out." She said, leaning up against the railing to the gazebo.

"Actually, you do," Amber said with a sly grin on her face.

"I picked up your bikini you had on your bed in your room." She said.

"I left it in one of Jason's guest rooms off the living room."

Damn her! Amber knew that Jessica would not have come if she knew that they were coming here to go swimming, or she was being set up on a date.

Instead of saying they were going swimming, or that Greg would be here, her sneaky cousin had told her they were going to a beach party. While Jessica was in the

22

shower, Amber went into Jessica's room and grabbed her bikini off the bed.

Jessica glanced at Greg standing next to her, with sexually spiked pheromones coming out of him like a hot summer night. She got the message loud and clear, and her eyes once again went down his slim waist and hips and straight to the bulge of his manhood, straining against his linen pants.

"Greg is here for three weeks, why don't you try to enjoy him?" Amber said teasingly. Jessica pulled Amber away from the men.

"You know for someone who says they are not trying to set me up on a date, this sure feels like a set up."

"And you being set up on a date is bad because of what?"

"I'm not that kind of girl, I don't jump in the bed with someone I just met."

"You didn't just meet him. And you know, you want to jump in the bed with him."

"Okay, so I want to get him in the bed, look at him, he is still so fine as ever. And I'm not that stupid to get involved with him again."

"Who said you have to get involved with him, you can choose to enjoy him or not, just go with the flow."

"Go with the damn flow? He could have a woman somewhere."

"He doesn't."

"How do you know?"

"Trust me, I know he doesn't." Amber stared at Jessica.

"You have given Brandon too much power over you, Jessica. Do not let what he did to you dictate your future happiness. You need to let go of all your hang-ups and start living and enjoying life. Because it's too damn short not to. Look at Greg." She said, nodding her head in the direction of the men.

"He is one handsome, eligible catch, and from the way he keeps looking at you I'd say he still has feelings for you. What is the worst thing that could happen? You end up having a good time while you're here, whatever it may be."

Jessica followed Amber's gaze. Yes, Greg was a sight to see, and that scared her. She had a problem of falling in love too easily.

She wore her heart and feelings on her sleeves. Jessica did not want to make the same mistakes she had made before in her past or send Greg the wrong messages. She did not want a long line of men coming in and out her life while she tried to find the right man for her.

"Amber I didn't come to North Carolina to find a man."

"I can understand that, but you will draw more attention to yourself if you don't join us. Greg may just sit out with you Jessica; that's the man he is.

Act like Greg doesn't have an effect on you, and there will be no pressure."

"It's a little too late for that," Jessica responded with a trembling chuckle, "well you do whatever you want to Jessica, you can play, or you can sit it out. But I'm going swimming." Amber marched back towards the men. Jessica became frustrated with Amber for pointing out the truth.
It has been two years since she'd been with a man, and it took sexy ass Greg to remind her of that hard ass fact. She went back over to the group.

"Seems like Amber has me all set, I'll go in and change now," she said and headed for the house.

Greg watched as Jessica went into the house to change into her swimsuit. He sat and reflected on the exchange they just had, never has a woman affected him as much as this one.

Jessica had him hook-line-and-sinker twenty years ago and seeing her here tonight face to face only made him realize that not only did she steal his heart so long ago, but she still had a hold on it to this day.

He had given up ever finding Jessica or seeing her again, he had gone on with his life, putting all his feelings away he had for her. Then to run into her again after so long was like a breath of fresh air. But he also knew that he had issues at home and getting involved with Jessica would not be a good idea at the moment, he thought to himself. As he walked into the house to change into his swimwear, Greg knew that no matter what he could not let Jessica get away this time...

Greg knew that he had made a mistake all those years ago and even broken her heart. But to run into her like this all these years later, he took it as his second chance to make things right. But will he be able to get Jessica to understand? And will she even give him the chance to explain to her that he still had feelings for her?

And if Jessica would have him, he wanted to make her his wife. But he had to first get over the issues that he still carried around with him.

Greg changed and returned to the group outside, with a plan to win Jessica back, he was gonna do whatever it took to get the love of his life back. No matter what, at least he hoped he could.

By the time Jessica came back outside, Amber, Jason, and Greg were already in the water acting like kids. Jessica stood at the edge of the water watching them and her mind wandered on about how she would love to wake up to the beach in her backyard every day.

"Jessica!"

Jessica's skin tingled at the sound of Greg's voice, and just the sight of his body coming out of the water as he came towards her. When he reached the shoreline, he reached out his hand to her. His teeth glistened in the twilight as he smiled and his eyes looked at her with appreciation and approval as they roamed over her body, clad in a dark blue bikini.

Jessica was glad she worked out and kept her body in shape. She ran towards him, placed her hand in his and let him lead her into the water.

Once in the water all her doubts and inhibitions seemed to fade away as they joined Amber and Jason who were waiting for them. They immediately started a game of water frisbee and water tag. Every time Greg touched her, she wanted to kiss him and make love to him.

After a light dinner on the back deck of Jason's house, Jason and Amber excused themselves and went into the house. Leaving Greg and Jessica alone.

"Would you like to take a walk, Jessica?"

"I guess. A walk would be nice. I want to enjoy as much of this beautiful beach as I can. There are no moonlit beaches in Ohio as you know."

"That's why I love going to the islands whenever I get a chance, you can be on the beach in minutes." Greg left his seat and came around to her side of the table and helped her from her chair.

"I would love to live on one," she said, as she took his hand. They walked along the beach away from Jason's house, talking and enjoying the breeze coming off the water. They walked hand in hand along the water's edge.

Chapter 5

Greg stopped and turned her around, to face him pulled her close to him, and wrapped his arms around her. He gazed down into her eyes.

"Would you mind if I kissed you, Jessica?"

Jessica's tongue darted from her mouth to lick her lips. It was a reflex motion in response to the heat that swept through her like fire. While her lower body throbbed with life and the excitement of the heavy flood of fluids heading down to settle, disturbingly at her vagina. Greg took her silence as an invitation and lowered his head. Jessica looked at Greg and moaned as his soft lips brushed hers, causing a tingling sensation all over her body. He tightened his arms around her and bent his knees slightly, and aligning his erection perfectly with her vagina, the shock of his arousal pressing into her feminine softness, sent a sharp gasp from her throat.

Greg took the opportunity to slide his tongue deep into her sweet mouth. Greg deepened the kiss; Jessica could do nothing but give into the moment. He was sucking the fight right out of her.

She wrapped her arms around his neck and kissed him with a hunger she didn't know she had. Forgotten were her inhibitions, her vow to let another man get close to her, her promise not to get involved with any man much less this man, and her oath to not wear her heart and feelings on her sleeve anymore, as their tongues danced around each other biting, teasing, capturing, and releasing until the sounds coming from them seemed to become one with each other.

Yes, Jessica wanted to get with him tonight and make love to him again, to feel his hands on her body once again. To have him so deep inside her that she forgets all her problems. To have him taste her the way only he knew how.

"Jessica..."

A warm delicious shudder ran through her body as he spoke her name. No man has ever spoken her name with such passion, such eroticism.

"So delish," Greg whispered in her ear as his lips trailed soft kisses across her cheek, over her chin and down her neck. His large hands were restless as he caressed and squeezed her sensitive breast.

Jessica was on fire. Jessica's skin sizzled wherever Greg touched her, and the wetness gathering in her panties was a sure sign she wanted him.

When Greg's lips wandered down the valley between her breast and the tip of his tongue lapped salaciously at one of her nipples, a wave of electrical currents went through Jessica's body and settled between her legs.

Jessica tried squeezing her thighs together to stop the uncontrollable throbbing of her pussy muscles.

Greg thrust gently against her, increasing the intensity of her need.
She was on the verge of exploding. Jessica had never experienced such wantonness, such yearning, not even during her moment of intercourse with Brandon. She thought their sex life was nothing to shout about, but they had a son to raise and protect, and for him, she'd put up with the lack of passion she knew she should have been experiencing when making love with her husband.
She'd been willing to go without the passion, until she found out Brandon was cheating on her, she came back to the present.

"No!"
With one thrust, Jessica pushed herself out of Greg's arms and started to run down the beach.

Jessica stopped, put her hands to her chest and took deep gulps of air, trying to desperately bring her senses back under control.

"Jessica, I'm sorry did I do something wrong to upset you? I thought this... what we shared was mutual; please forgive me if I have offended you. It wasn't my intentions. I just wanted to kiss you, have wanted to kiss you ever since I saw you standing on the beach against the sunset." Jessica heard the perplexity in Greg's voice. He'd asked her if he could kiss her. She hadn't said he couldn't, and when he had taken her silence as a yes, she didn't protest. In fact, she urged him on, melting into him, and giving him permission to relish her.

"I'm sorry, Greg" she said.

"It's not you." Greg walked over to her, he watched her with keenly observant eyes.

"It's not you. Such a pathetic overused phrase. If it's not me, then what is it?" Jessica felt so vulnerable, and helpless, the magnetism of this irresistible man.

"I haven't been with a man since after my separation from my husband." She said, shaking off the embarrassing thought.

"It has been two years since I have let another man get this close to me."

"So, what we just did scared you then?"
She nodded.

"We just met; I don't know you. I
shouldn't be..." Her voice trailed off.

"You mean you shouldn't be having these
feelings, so soon. I understand Jessica, I feel
the same way. I thought that all my feelings
for you were buried away somewhere. But
seeing you face to face has proven that they
are still strong and that I am still in love
with you."
Greg took Jessica in his arms and hugged
her tight.

"Will you allow us to get to know each
other again?" She thought for a moment.

"Yes!" she said.
Jessica and Greg spent the next three weeks
of their vacation getting to know each other
again.
They spent time at the boardwalk, dining on
sushi and other seafood dishes at the Saigon
Bay.

Holding hands as they walked along the
boardwalk bridge. They took romantic rides
along the water on the paddle boats.

Every day she spent with Greg he took
down the wall she had built around her

heart so well. They enjoyed their nights at The Dirty Thirty Club, dancing, and drinking. They agreed that they were both not ready to be in a serious relationship at the moment and agreed to just take it one day at a time.

Jessica told Greg about how her life was for the past twenty years, all the heartache and pain that she went through after they broke up. They talked about the pain she had for losing their baby. But most of all they talked about the feelings they still shared for each other.

But Jessica knew that when she left North Carolina that the memories of what took place between her and Greg would be just that cherished memories of the time they shared. Because she was in a situation with Winston and didn't want to hurt his feelings. Because Winston was a very nice guy.

They weren't serious or anything just friends and he had made it known that he wanted her. Winston was sexy in his own way he was stocky built, light brown complexion, with the most kissable lips and beautiful smile. He was just too much of a flirt for Jessica, but she liked him. Even though Jessica and Winston had never had sex, she knew that he wanted too. But she wasn't ready for that yet with him.

Two days before they were to leave North Carolina they returned to the boardwalk to enjoy ice cream and lunch at the Ninety-Nine ice cream shoppe. And dinner and drinks at the Fire Water. Greg took Jessica to dinner on the beach on their last night in North Carolina. They watched the sunset, as it became a multitude of colors, before disappearing.

They walked along the beach hand in hand, laughing and enjoying the last moments of their vacation together.

"Do you ever want to get married again?" Greg asked. Jessica thought about that for a while.

"Yes, I would love to get married again. I actually loved being a wife, mother and taking care of the house. The problem was the person
I was married to."

CHAPTER 6

"**I'm** sorry I wasn't there for you
Jessica, I'm sorry that you had to go through
what you went through these past years...
Why didn't you come to me? Why didn't you
call me?"

"Because I always thought you were with
someone, that you had gotten
married."

"Jessica even if I was with someone, and
you came to me I would have left her for
you." Jessica laughed at Greg, "You know
that you would not have left a woman that
you were seeing for me."

"Jessica, I knew back then that you were
the one for me, I was just too damn stupid

to do anything about it until it was too late. I let you get away from me and I don't intend to let you get away again. I will not let another twenty years go by without you in my life."

Greg knew he had to make Jessica understand how he felt about her. Even though he was not ready for a serious relationship right now, he knew that he could not let Jessica leave North Carolina without her knowing that he still loved her. That he wanted her in his life for here on out. Jessica needed to know that she was his life and that he had missed her all those years of them being apart.

She needed to know that he wanted her to have his babies, and that he was also sad about the baby they had lost so long ago. She deserved to be taken care of and treated the right way by a man. And he planned to be that man, the man that gave her what she needed most. And that was all the love that he could give... He placed his mouth so close to Jessica's, barely touching their lips together.

His breath slowly crept out as it intertwined with Jessica's. The soft touch of his large hands flowing down her face, her neck and onto her breast made her internally beg for more.

He pinched and sucked her erect dark brown nipples sending a sea of shock waves through them both, and down to her clit. She wanted him, and Greg knew it, they both did. This was it.

This was going to be the night that Jessica had been waiting for; for the past three weeks, the man of her dreams, the man she had loved for twenty years.

His sweat and saliva buried Jessica's pussy as he lifted his head, inserting a finger. She was scared and nervous as her body trembled, thinking if this was right? Should they be doing this? Wondering if Greg would call her or see her again after he has had his way, or would he just do his bid and leave?

Tears flowed from Jessica's eyes down her cheeks, as she felt the tip of his tongue on her clit and inside her pussy, Greg would love her good like he's always done before in the past, but her head was telling her not to let him get to close to her heart again.

Several hours later as they lie in each other's arms. "Can I ask you a personal question?"

"Yes, sure."

"Does he make you cum every night? Do your toes curl before his curl? Does he pull your hair while hitting that delicious pussy from the back and tell you that this shit is his pussy?" He asked moving closer to her.

"Does he make you scream?"

"Greg don't do this."

"Just answer the question Jessica."

"Does he?"

"No!" She said loudly.

"What the hell you mean No?" Greg looked at her with concern.

"We've never had sex before." She said.

"Damn, Jessica that is something that you should be experiencing every night. What if I told you that I want you and I won't stop until I convince you to be mine?"

Her vacation was the best she has had in a long ass time. Now that she was back home in her own house, back to her old life. But ready to take the next steps in her career, with her cake business.

Jessica sat back and reflected on every memory that she and Greg had made in North Carolina the past few weeks; they will always be etched in her heart.

Jessie didn't know what the outcome would be between her and Greg, she didn't know if she wanted there to be an outcome or not. All she knew at the moment was that her feelings for him had manifested and taken over her heart.

She knew that no man will ever be able to come in and make her feel the way that he did. For so long she has been so unsatisfied with sex because no one has ever been able to make her feel the way that Greg has.

Jessica now realized that all these years she has been comparing other men to Greg, and they have never measured up to his standards sexually or as a man. And now that she has gotten another taste of him, Jessica knew that she wanted no other man but him...

Two weeks later someone rang her doorbell.

"I wonder who that is." She said, looking out the window.

"Oh my gosh, it couldn't be. Greg is at my door." She said. Jessica let him in.

"Hi Jessie." He said.

"I just came by to check to see if you were alright, I haven't heard from you since we left North Carolina." Jessica stared at Greg with so much passion in her eyes that she knew he could feel it seeping through her pores.

"I have been busy with my shop and my son." She said, Greg took her face in his hands and lowered his head to kiss her. His breath smelled like honey. It was so intoxicating.

"What if I told you that ever since we made love in North Carolina, all I could think about, dream about where you? You are going to be mine, and I won't stop until you are."

CHAPTER 7

"**You** don't mean that."

"What if I told you that your other friend is temporary, that he is just taking up space in your life, until I make you realize that you are going to belong to me?"

"Oh shit... Greg–"

"Answer me Jessica." Greg whispered close to her ear.

"We can't do this. Greg stop."

"You don't want me to stop, now do you Jessica?" His voice was so damn sexy, damn near hypnotizing.

"Your body is speaking to me; it has always spoken to me, Jessica. I know that you are unhappy and unsatisfied. And I want to bring happiness and that smile that I remember back into your life."

"I could bend you over the side of this couch right now, just pull your dress up and bend you over right now." He said forcefully.

"Tell me Jessica what you want me to do to you? Do you want me to make you scream while I lick that pussy? Tell me that you want me to touch you that you want to cum in my mouth." Yes! Yes! Yes! She wanted to say out loud so damn badly. Her eyes rolled to the back of her head as Greg sucked and licked her neck as his tongue rotated in a circular motion as he moved down toward her breast.

Jessica felt her nipples become erect and her clit started to pulsate as he ran his hands down her stomach. Greg whispered in her ear.

"Tell me what you want me to do Jessica. You want me to eat that pussy the way you like?"

Oh! Yes! Yes! Yes! She wanted to scream out loud so damn badly, but her heart told her to slow her roll. She didn't know what his intentions were. Is she just someone he wants to fuck, or is she someone he wants in his life permanently?

Greg bent Jessica over the arm of the couch pulled her dress up and got down on his knees and tenderly began to open her silky folds and hungrily licked at her pussy from the back.

"Yes! Yes! Yes!" Jessica screamed, This is what I'm talking about, this is what I have missed for twenty damn years... She thought to herself. Greg ate her pussy for so long that she could not cum anymore, she thought. Greg stood up and put on a condom before he entered her, Jessica let out a sigh of relief because she just loved it when he was inside her, and it was like coming home after a long day of work.

"Am I fucking you right?" Greg whispered in her ear as he placed his hand in her hair and pulled her head back and began to kiss her. Jessica has never let a guy kiss her after he ate her out but that's the difference between Greg and any other man.

Greg had a control over Jessica that no man has ever had, not a bad kind of control but a control that has Jessica doing whatever he asks of her. Without him actually, asking her to do it. Greg has that confidence of a man in control of everything that he does. Greg fucked Jessica so damn good it had her cumming so hard. He knew how she liked it she never had to tell him how to fuck her or suck her because he knew how.

He grabbed Jessica's shoulders and pushed hungrily deep into her love cave, as he desperately sexed her brains out; banging and pumping making Jessica want more. Greg began to tease her with his dick, Jessica hated when he did this, it drove her crazy. But at the same time Jessica loved it. Greg caressed and squeezed her breast from behind and it felt like heaven.

"Greg... I can't do this, this isn't right."

"Fuck that nigga you claim to like; he can't do what I can for you. He can't make you feel the way I can. You deserve to be teased, pleased, and pleasured. And damn it I plan to do just that."

"Greg!" She cried, tears falling from her eyes.

"Please, Greg."
Greg picked Jessica up and carried her to her room; he took her dress off and

continued where he left off. He fucked her so long and hard. Greg did things to Jessica that have never been done before.

"Marry me Jessica!"

That following weekend Greg came to her shop, "I just wanted to see you before I went into work today and ask if you would take a ride with me later when you closed up for the day."

Jessica smiled, as he walked up to the counter.

"Sure, I would love to take a ride with you later. What did you have planned, for later?" She asked.

"Nothing special just wanted to spend some time with you, that's all."

She looked around her shop and said, "since its slow today I can close an hour early today, so I should be off around four-thirty."

"Okay I will be at your place around five-thirty to pick you up." Jessica smiled and nodded her head ok, as she waited on a customer, Greg winked at her and left the shop.

The day was quite warm, for the beginning of October the bright sunshine beating down as his red Nova zipped along the country road. Greg watched her out the corner of his eye, appreciating the short skirt Jessica was wearing.

He always got a twinge in the pit of his stomach when he thought of her; the way her legs wrapped around him when they made love, the feel of her skin, the taste of her, and the smell of her.

Greg felt himself growing just a bit from thinking about her. Jessica was daydreaming about the night they had just shared. She turned to look at him, and he at her. They smiled at each other, knowing instinctively what the other was thinking.

Jessica glanced down and noticed the bulge in his pants. A big grin spread across her face as she thought about him. She turned and slid across the seat towards Greg.

Placing her lips close to his ear, she whispered how much she liked the things they had done together the week before. Jessica reached down to rub him with her palm. Through his jeans, she felt him push up to her hand slightly. She touched his ear with the tip of her tongue, tracing the edge all the way from the bottom of the lobe to the top, then dipping slightly to the inside.

Greg shivered, as a growl escaped his lips, and he tightened his grip on the steering wheel. She unbuttoned his jeans and slowly pulled down his zipper. She was toying with his ear, teasing with her tongue, nipping lightly with her teeth.
Her breath in his ear was wonderful as was the pressure of her hand on his swelling dick.

"Raise your hips, Greg," Jessica whispered.

Greg gladly obliged, and she slid his jeans down over his hips to give her access to him. She began to caress him with her hand, as she kissed downward, on the side of his neck, in the hollow where his shoulder began, and still downward.

She unbuttoned his shirt, kissing the skin as it was exposed. Jessica took his nipple lightly between her teeth, running the tip of her tongue over it as he took in a sharp breath. Greg slowed a bit, unable to concentrate on his driving and what her hands and mouth were doing to him at the same time. He placed his right hand on her hair, caressing her lovingly.

She continued to kiss his warm skin, slowly working her way downward, toward his straining erection. Jessica took him in her hand again and held him while she lowered her head and flicked her tongue against the tip of his dick. Soft, feathery, teasing, little licks caused him to shudder.

His hand still in her hair, Greg pushed her head down. He pushed himself into her hot mouth. Jessica eagerly took him in. She swirled her tongue around him, licking, sucking him. His fingers tightening in her hair, he pushed her down even further until his entire erection disappeared in her mouth. Greg groaned loudly, gripping the wheel and her hair tighter. Jessica began to pull back, all the way to the tip, only to slide her lips down again. Finding it harder to drive, he slowed even more. As Jessica pumped up and down, with one hand she massaged his balls, rubbing and squeezing lightly with the other. Greg took his foot off the gas all together, looking for a place to stop. He found what he was looking for; a dirt drive, almost hidden amongst the trees.

He followed it a ways, back into the woods, until he came to a small clearing. He stopped the car, turned off the engine and leaned back in his seat, enjoying the feel of her lips and mouth on his candy muscle.

Jessica started moving faster, taking all of him. He watched himself slide in and out of her mouth, such a beautiful sight.

Chapter 8

He felt the stirring of his release building within him. He was squirming in the seat, holding her head in his hands, her hair tangled in his fingers. Greg watched as he disappeared in her mouth, again and again, his erection glistening with her saliva.

God, her mouth felt wonderful on him. Unable to contain himself any longer, Greg pulled her mouth away as he let out a growl, grabbing a towel and filling it with his essence.

When his breathing returned to normal, she started to caress him with her fingertips once again. Almost instantly, he began to swell.

His hands wandered from her hair down to her back, around her side, over her hip and back up again.

Greg wanted badly to see her naked body in the sunlight, to feel her with his hands and taste her again. He pulled her up off of him and, looking into her eyes, kissed her passionately, tasting himself on her lips, feeling the softness of her mouth with his. His tongue parted her lips, insisting on exploring her inner warmth. He thought first of her mouth and later, of other, more intimate regions. Jessica moaned softly, pulling him tightly into her embrace. He wanted badly to lay her on the seat and make love to her but knew that there was not enough room to move around like he wanted.

"Get out of the car" he told her. Greg reached into the back seat, retrieved a blanket, walked to the front of the car, and spread it on the hood.
Greg reached out for her and Jessica stepped into his embrace, loving the feel of his body as he pulled her close. He kissed

her again, taking his time to taste every inch of her mouth before pulling back slightly to kiss her cheeks, her nose, and her eyelids.

Tracing his tongue along the line of her jaw, kissing, and caressing her face with his mouth. His hands played across her back, massaging, lightly squeezing her, his hands drifting down to cup both her ass cheeks, pulling her even closer.

Jessica could feel the contours of his body, every bulge, especially the one pressing into her most intimate place. Greg was so very hard again, and she was on fire for him. He tugged her short skirt down over her hips, then her top came off over her head and Jessica was left standing in nothing but her bra and panties.

Greg loved how the white lace looked against her smooth light brown skin.

"Turn around," he said softly. Jessica turned to face the car. Greg stepped directly behind her, placed his hands on her shoulders, and began a tortuously slow exploration of her body with his hands and mouth.

"Don't tease me Greg, Please."

"I told you before teasing is pleasing, and I plan to tease and please you for here on out." Kissing her shoulders, the back of her neck, and then let his fingertips glide down her back to the top of her lacy panties. He massaged her ass through the cloth and moved his hands around to the front. Pulling the full length of her body against his, pressing his lips to her neck once again. His hands moved up to cup both her breasts, bringing a moan from her. Jessica pushed her lace-covered bottom tightly against his rock-hard dick. Greg gently squeezed her breast through the lace, feeling her nipples straining to be free.

He was glad to oblige, undoing the hook and letting the wisp of lace fall away. Jessica kept pushing herself against him, moaning softly, as he thoroughly massaged her breast, finally taking the hard sensitive nipples in his fingers and squeezing. She groaned loudly, melting into him. Trying to keep his control, Greg backed away from her a bit and told her to bend over and put her hands on the hood of the car.

She quickly obliged. This was of no help to his composure, seeing Jessica bent over, nothing covering her cheeks but a thin strip of white lace. Kneeling behind her, Greg placed his hands on her hips and let them roam over her ass, pausing at her thighs, and continuing down the entire length of her legs.

Jessica wiggled with anticipation as he reached for the top of her panties and began ever-so-slowly to pull them over her hips, kissing, biting, and sucking the exposed flesh. He moved his mouth slowly down her legs, licking his way down, kissing the sensitive places behind her knees.

Lifting her feet, first one, then the other, as he removed her panties. Jessica felt as if she would faint when Greg spread her legs and placed his tongue on her inner thigh. He brushed his fingers over her, touching her with his tongue, causing her to shiver. Pushing her thighs further apart, he finally touched the tip of his tongue to her already swollen lips, tasting the wetness that was beginning to drip from her.

Her cries of pleasure mixed with the sounds of birds singing in the trees as he entered her with his tongue, sucking and licking up the moisture, inhaling her natural perfume.

Her knees were getting weaker as he licked and sucked her lips, moving up the crease between her ass, lightly biting with his teeth, causing her to quiver and beg him to take her. Greg was determined to take his time, to bring her to the brink again and again, and then give her the most intense release possible.

He licked and sucked his way back to the entrance between her hot pussy lips and slipped his tongue in once again as far as he could.

Another loud cry escaped Jessica, and she pushed back against him. He held her firm and moved his mouth further towards her clit, using the tip of his tongue to lick all around without actually touching it.

Panting, gasping for breath, Jessica begged him to give her the release she needed badly. Greg continued his slow, methodical consumption of her, getting more aroused by the minute. He finally touched her clit with his tongue and sucked it between his lips, tugging lightly on it. He could feel her orgasm rising to the surface, so he pulled away, stepping back from her.

Jessica stood and turned toward him, reaching to pull him to her. He backed her against the hood of the car, kissed her passionately and pushed her down onto the hood. She lay back, feeling the warmth of the car on her back through the blanket, the warm sun beating down on her naked body.

Greg quickly shed his clothes and leaned over her, again tasting her sweet mouth, caressing her breast, feeding the smoldering fire that was inside her. Jessica grasped his head in her hands and pulled his mouth to her breast. He nibbled first one hard nipple, then the other. Finally, unable to contain his need of her any longer, Greg placed the tip of his straining dick at her hot, wet entrance between her legs, rubbing it back and forth along her lips, covering him with her juices. With a single, swift thrust, he was inside her. Jessica cried out, writhing beneath him, pushing her hips upward to meet his as he began moving within her, trying to go slowly, but finding it impossible to hold back.

The sun, the birds, the warm afternoon breezes; all went unnoticed as he slid

himself in and out of her, both of them lost
in each other, consumed by the passion.
Moving faster now, feeling her orgasm rising
once again, as well as his own, Greg stood,
pulling Jessica to the edge of the hood so
that he was standing between her legs. He
lifted her legs, placed her feet at his
shoulders and slid even deeper inside her.
Her whimpers turned into cries of intense,
almost painful pleasure as an exquisite
orgasm overtook Jessica.

Her contracting feminine muscles
gripped Greg tightly again and again,
sending him over the edge with her.
Greg filled her with his manly juices.
here.

Chapter 9

Greg came over every other day
for two weeks after he sexed her on the
hood of the car. Greg asked Jessica to marry
him again. Jessica just looked at him
because she knew that he wasn't serious. At
least she thought he wasn't.

But every day Greg was tearing the walls
down around her heart. And she was scared
of that because at the same time Jessica's
feelings for Greg were getting stronger and
stronger.

Greg showed her what a real man was in
every aspect of the word, and Jessica began
to crave that. Two weeks before

Thanksgiving Greg was sitting at her kitchen table, "come here Jessica."

"Why?"

"Just come here." Jessica was hesitant to go because she knew what was about to happen, this was not the first time Greg has taken her on the table. She went to him in a trance because that's just how he made her feel when he was around.

Greg pulled her pants and panties down and lifted her onto the table.

"Spread your legs." Greg requested moving to sit in front of Jessica at the table in a chair; He proceeded to put a small towel around his neck so that he wouldn't get his shirt messy.

Jessica did what he asked.

"Mmmm, that pussy looks so damn good and ready for me." He licked his lips as he salivated at the sight of Jessica's hot steaming pussy on display. As she spread her legs even further giving Greg an even better view. He licked his lips again as he slowly got into position like a lion ready to take down his prey, slowly moving in for the kill.

"Oh, damn that pussy is hot too. Tell me Jessica baby what you want me to do."

"Greg, this isn't right, I can't talk dirty to you."

"Shit Jessica, a closed mouth don't get fed. Now tell me what you want Jessica." He said as he opened his mouth and began to eat her pussy. His tall body was sitting in front of Jessica in a chair with his head and face so deep in her pussy. Jessica's vagina was throbbing over time and was long overdue for some tender loving care like this.

"What do you want me to do Jessica?" He asked again.

"I want you to make this pussy cum, baby."

"Mmmm, is that right?"
He asked as he repositioned himself back in the chair in front of Jessica. She felt like he was placing her in some kind of trance or was hypnotizing her.

Greg stuck his tongue so far up in Jessica's vagina that it made her scream, Jessica loved the way he ate her pussy it was like no other, he had this way that he did things to Jessica to get her to do what he wanted her to do.

Jessica tried to get away, but he kept pulling her back to his mouth and tongue. The tingling sensation in her body was a feeling that Jessica hadn't felt in a long ass time.

"Your pussy is so damn good Jessica; I don't want to stop eating it."
That made her pussy wetter than it already was.

"This pussy is so damn juicy and wet, damn, how this pussy get so wet, like this?" He asked, all Jessica could do was moan in response.
Greg began to tease Jessica for a while, she hated when he did this.

"Why are you teasing me?" She asked.

"Teasing is pleasing, and you deserve to be teased. Your body needs to be seduced, touched and caressed in ways that it deserves, it should be catered to."

After he devoured Jessica's honey pot he stood up and fucked Jessica so well she had tears rolling down her face. Never has any man been able to make Jessica feel the way this man does.
Not even in her eight years of marriage did Jessica's husband make her feel this way. He fucked Jessica so good that her pussy was

spilling out her juices all over the table and floor.

It was the best feeling ever.

It was a Monday night, and he hadn't seen or spoken to Jessica in over a week. Greg knew that he had left a lasting impression on her, but damn she left an even bigger impression on him. Damn she hasn't even made an attempt to call me or come over. The intrigue was getting to him, as he made his dinner Greg stared out the window into the distance, listening to the storm outside his kitchen window.

The sky grew dark as the raindrops slapped against his windowpane, as Greg's thoughts drifted to the last time he was with Jessica; wondering if he had missed his opportunity to make her his. He was having dinner with his ex-girlfriend but thinking about Jessica, Greg missed the way her skin felt, the smell of her, and her essence. Damn he missed her. The way her body responds to his touch.

Greg thought about how his large masculine hands reached down and picked her up and sat her sexy ass on the table. Separating her legs, as he licked her pussy slowly and gently the way she likes it, sucking on her clit and going deep into her hot furnace with his tongue. He gently lifted her legs and brought them back to her shoulders as he massaged the backs of her thighs with his hands. With her ass just about facing the ceiling he placed his long-wet tongue in between her ass. Her legs began to tremble as Greg licked up and down, like he was cleaning his plate.

Greg loved making her moan, her moans were like listening to the soothing sounds of the rippling ocean as he buried his face in her pussy; eagerly fucking her with his tongue. Realizing that every move he made was driving her insane as she tried to hold her composure. Breathing heavily her chest bounced up and down that he thought she would pass out. With his mouth to her opening, Greg sucked gently then quickly moved to her throbbing clit.

"Shit! Shit! Shit!" she screamed. He then realized that no man had ever done or made her feel anything like that before. And Jessica was gonna learn that day that he was not the average man. As his dick grew a mile a minute, Greg wasn't the kind of man to just hit the pussy without loving the pussy first. He loved pussy, not all pussy, but most pussy. But Jessica's pussy he wanted to please and devour and love for a lifetime... He came back to the present, looked over at his date and realized that he was gonna miss his chance to be with Jessica because he couldn't make his mind up.

Chapter 10

Sitting on the couch Jessica was talking to Shayla on the phone.

"I don't know what the outcome is going to be for me and Greg; I don't even know how he really feels about me."

"Maybe you should ask him."

"Sometimes I feel like I am just someone to pass his time with. All I know is that my feelings have become so strong for him and it hurts knowing that I allowed him to get this close to me again. Something in my heart keeps telling me that I never should've loved him, but I just couldn't help it." She said.

"I understand, honey things will work out."

"Shayla it has taken me four years to build a wall around my heart and it only took him six months to tear it down."

"Jessie, I know you feel that you love this man, but you have to see that he is playing with you and your emotions. You need to take a time out you have a lot on your plate with your marriage coming to an end, your new bakery just opening and raising your son. Honey you need some time for yourself right now. Without a man." Shayla told her.

"Will I ever be able to trust again? Will I ever be able to open my heart up again and let someone in again?"

"Maybe you should take time out and do you for a while, not worry about a man right now. Your family vacation is coming up soon why don't you think about going on that cruise with them."

"Just thinking about him makes my body warm all over, not just because he knows how to put it down in the bedroom. But because I thought there had been a connection between us..."

"But you just got your court date for your divorce, so you are very emotional anyway right now. Just take a time out and you will be able to see things clearly."

"But I thought that I really meant something to him because after all he had asked me to marry him three times already."

"Maybe it was because you were in the heat of the moment when he asked you." Shayla said. Jessica laughed at the thought of Greg asking her to marry him while in the middle of having sex.

"Hmm, maybe that was all it was after all. The heat of the moment talking..."

"Listen, I have to get to work just think about what I said Jessica, okay. Love you. Talk to you later."

"I will Shayla because you're right, I do need a time out. Love you to talk to you later, bye."

It had been two months, and still Jessica hadn't heard a word from Greg. She didn't want to call him and ask him why he hasn't called or came by.

Jessica didn't want to seem like a desperate woman in need of a man that was not hers. But Jessica felt like she deserved some kind of answers as to why he kept disappearing from her life weeks at a time. Jessica understood the fact that they don't share the same last name or have kids together, but she allowed him to lie up in her at night whenever he wanted to, while she pretended and believed that they could actually have a future together. She deserved some kind of explanation. She allowed this cycle to go on for a year, believing and hoping that he wanted to be with her.

As Jessica sat listening to her music and drinking a glass of Pink Moscato and thinking about what her friend had told her a few months back and she was ready to move on she thought. A knock at her door incited hopefulness. She hoped that it was Greg, on bended knee, telling her how sorry he was for not being around much, and spend the next thirty minutes trying to apologize for his lack of attention. She opened the door hoping that it was Greg, only to see her neighbor Tommy greeting her on the other side of the door; Jessica wished that she had not opened the door.

"Hey, Jessica. What have you been up to?"

"Listening to my music." she said. He stopped and tried to peek into her house.

"Want some company?"

"It's ten o'clock at night, Tommy." She said.

"So, you have a curfew now?" He said with a smirk.

"Tommy, what possessed you to knock on my door at this time of night thinking that you were coming in my house?"

"I just noticed how down you've been lookin lately and thought I would offer my company, to help cheer you up." When she first moved in, Tommy was the first person she met. He was nice and always willing to look out for her and her house when she was gone.

He wanted more than to be her friendly neighbor, but Jessica had no interest in him any other way. But unfortunately, he was a relentless critter.

"I appreciate that, Tommy, but I'm tired and ready for bed, I have work in the morning."

"Well, I wanted you to know that you are not alone."

Jessica was offended by his reference to her absent social life. And a little pissed that he noticed how often her doorbell rang. Jessica didn't feel like she had to make excuses for herself, but Tommy's insinuations about her made Jessica a little uneasy. She smiled and shut her door in his face. She returned to the couch and her music.

When she didn't notice her phone ring that night, she realized that she had been sitting on the couch staring off into space and not even listening to her music; the hope of Greg's name and number flashing across her screen had disappeared a long time ago. She was done waiting on a man.

Jessica made the decision to move on, concentrate on her bakery and her son. While in bed tossing and turning, her doorbell rings, walking to the door Jessica looks at the time on the stove top. Wondering who the hell was at her door this late. When she opened her door and noticed Greg's tall frame standing in her doorway, it literally took her breath away.

Jessica held her breath as her eyes took in this fine ass specimen before her and her pussy immediately began to get moist. The last thing Jessica expected was Greg knocking at her door at one o'clock in the morning, especially after not seeing him for over two months.

Still, her breath found it hard to come out as her eyes gazed at how fine he looked dressed in black slacks, with a short sleeve powder blue button-down opened up over a black tank top with a black Kango turned around backwards on his head and his gold chain around his neck.

"What are you doing here?" She asked.

"Let me in Jessica." She opened the door for him. He spread his arms and like a love-struck fool she walked into his arms as if nothing has happened. He licked his lips and kissed her and gazed over her body.

"I wanted to see you Jessica. And talk to you." His voice danced off his lips and slid between her inner thighs.

"We have nothing to talk about, I haven't seen or heard from you in over two months.

"That's what I wanted to talk to you about."

"Greg save it, you must be horny or something." He bit his bottom lip and smiled. And yes, her damn knees quivered, but Jessica stood her ground and folded her arms over her chest, like him biting' his lip didn't do anything to her.

"Like I said save it."

"C'mon, Jessica. It's not like that and you know it. But I'm not gonna lie just lookin at you standing there like that you sure look sexy and beautiful. But I did come to talk."

"About what? It's been two months Greg."

"I'm trying to move on."

"Is that right, Jessica?" Within seconds, she was in his arms and his lips were on her neck. She tried to pull away, but his lips met hers and Jessica's words were lost in translation. His actions showed her that they were over, but his lips said something else as he kissed her neck and whispered dirty little nothings in her ear.

All Jessica could think about is how his lips tasted when they touched hers. Before she knew what was going on their clothes hit the floor and they were in her house trying to make it to her bedroom. Jessica felt like a fool for letting him do this to her all the time. But as soon as he put his hands on her skin, she was his.

Jessica was his for him to lie inside her once again, and for him to play with her emotions all over again. But nonetheless, in that moment, she needed him. Jessica needed to feel him, to hold him, to feel a man strong and as sexy as Greg to sex her right and to assure her that she deserved to be pleased the way she needed to be pleased. And Greg was the only man that knew how to do that.

At least for the moment. "You can't stay here, Greg."

"We can't do this," Jessica said as she wrapped her legs around his waist to keep him from walking out the door. As she tilted her head back Greg sucked the space under her chin and below her ear, knowing that this drove her crazy.

"You know you missed me, Jessica" he said in her ear, as he stroked her body with his hands, he slowly satisfied Jessica and made her reach her climax.

A task that only Greg knew too well. She needed for his dick to do to her what she lies in bed all alone hoping that he'd come back and do. Jessica was only fooling herself if she thought that she had any kind of say over what was gonna happen the moment he knocked on her door.

As soon as he knocked on her door, their fates were sealed and they were destined to lie in her bed and soil her sheets with their love juices, and Jessica begging for more- and Greg knew it.

She was just thankful that her son had went to go stay with Brandon for a week or she would not had let him in.

Chapter 11

Twenty years ago, they had stolen each other's hearts and somehow became each other's drug and it felt damn good to get high off him. But Jessica couldn't keep playing the fool. Especially to a man she never should've loved a second time around.

"Are you seeing someone else Greg, is that why you don't call me or come by for weeks at a time?" While he dropped that sexy innocent smile, and being playful at first, trying to go for round two, as they lay naked in the bed at three in the morning. He sat up and bit his bottom lip.

"You just had to go and spoil the mood, huh?" I sat up and put my night shirt on.

"Greg, we have to discuss the reasons why you only show up when you want to get your dick wet, and how that is making me feel."

"Does it need to be right now?"

"If we don't talk about it now, then when?"

He shrugged his shoulders.

"Just don't want to mess up a good thing a second time. I don't want to wear out my welcome. I don't want you to get bored with me."

"How can I get tired of you, or bored with you, I love you with everything I have, and you act like you don't care."

"You don't think that I love you, Jessica?"

"No, I don't think you do. You never tell me that you love me, so no I don't think you do." Jessica knew that she ran the risk of ending a beneficial sexual relationship between them, but at this point she had to do what was best for her emotionally and mentally. It felt so good to feel him inside her, but it hurt like hell to watch him leave. Jessica was always left with sticky thighs and an emotional wreck. She was tired of crying over a man that didn't want her the way that she wanted him. At some point Jessica had to respect the woman that stared back at her in the mirror.

Here she was being delusional thinking that they might have something going when all he really wanted was a quick fucken nut. A year had passed since they had reconnected, and she was tired.

"Jessica, I do care about you but I'm just not ready for what you want from me right now. I'm not ready to be committed to you at this point in time."

"If you were not ready for a committed relationship then why did you ask me to marry you on more than one occasion? WHY!" She screamed at him. Greg looked at her with a confused look on his face.

"Jessica, I have never asked you to marry me." He said.

As she tried to keep the tears from falling, Jessica stood up and pointed to her front door.

"You need to leave then." He turned and got out of bed, put on his clothes. No more words were spoken between them as he walked out the front door.

Jessica was done with him; he had hurt her for the last time. Even though it hurt to walk away from him. She had to let him go; she didn't want the tears to fall but she could no longer take the pain he kept causing her.

When he walked out her door without saying goodbye, the tears slowly crept down her face. This time, when she lies in her bed, it wouldn't be with the man who turned her world upside down and made her fall back in love with him.

The following day Jessica was feeling so emotional and hurt by the way Greg had treated her the night before, as she wrote down her feelings in her journal, she decides to call Lynne and see if she wanted to have lunch because she needed to get her mind off of Greg...

Sometimes

Sometimes we see what we want to see.
Sometimes we hear what we want to hear.
Only to find out it was not what we thought
it was all along.
Sometimes we open our heart too soon.
Sometimes not soon enough.
Sometimes we verbalize our feelings before
we think them through, only to be
devastated, heartbroken and crushed from
the reality of the response that we receive.
Sometimes loving someone is best kept
locked away with the hope of one day they
will feel the same.
Sometimes the love you have for someone is
too much for them to accept.
Sometimes it's not enough at all.
Sometimes they are just not ready for what
you have to give.
Sometimes love is not what they want at all.
Sometimes their heart is just not ready to
receive the love you have to share.
Sometimes love is just not enough at all.
Sometimes...

Jessie.

Sitting across from Lynne at TGIF, having lunch and drinks.

"How are things between you and Greg?" Jessica wanted to talk about something else, but her sister would only keep asking until she told her. Jessica shrugged her shoulders and pursed her lips.

"It is what it is."

"What does that mean, Jessica?"

"I walked away from him; I had to put him out the other night. Plus, I saw him with a woman in his driveway one night, on my way home from the gym."
Lynne lifted her eyebrows in disbelief.

"What I'm surprised you had it in you to do it. I thought that you would keep up this crazy charade."

"What you mean charade?"

"How long did you think an affair with a man who you know doesn't want a relationship with you was gonna last? You should've never let him come back in the first place."

"The same can be said about you when you let your ex back in your life after he cheated on you, only to come back and do it all over again." Jessica didn't like her blatant disregard for her bruised feelings and emotions, and she paid no regard to her feelings.

"At some point every woman plays the fool some time in her life, but what can you do about it."
Lynne sucked her teeth and sipped her drink...

"Yes, they do but it doesn't mean that you continue to play the fool over a man that has shown you time and time again that you are just his fuck partner." Lynne said as she slammed her hand down hard on the table. Jessica loved her sister, but she forgets that she has a past of her own. Jessica wanted to apologize, because her sister was right, but she was hurt by her sister's words as well.

They parted ways without any more words. The rest of the day Jessica thought about calling Lynne and apologizing, but she wanted her to call first and apologize. When she got home to her empty house, she picked up the phone to call her.
When, a knock on her door interrupted

Jessica as always. Hoping that it was Lynne coming over to apologize with a bottle of Moscato she opened the door ready to apologize, it was not Lynne standing on the other side of the door, all thoughts of Lynne were put aside by the appearance of Greg's face. She put her phone down and rubbed her temples.

"What are you doing here?" For once she wasn't weak in the knees. Jessica's stance was firm and unwavering.

"Can I come in?" Damn, he looked so good. He always gave me the opportunity to see him in a shirt that caressed his upper body and showed off his muscles or pants that fit him to a tee.
Jessica could imagine herself grabbing his butt and just squeezing it. But she was ready for him.

"No, I have plans." She tried to shut the door in his face, but he held it before she had the chance.

"I'm not trying to spend the night. I just wanna talk about the other night."

"Why? You had a chance to talk the other night you walked out."

"No, you kicked me out."

She looked down at the hand that held her doorknob.

"Greg, I think you need to leave. I have things to do."

"You're not gonna let me explain?"

"You had plenty of time to explain. Plus, I see that you have moved on or maybe she has been around all this time."

"What are you talking about?"

"I saw you with some woman the other day and you looked all personal with each other.
So, you think that I'm supposed to stand here and let you tell me some bullshit story you came up with just because you wanted to?"

He bit his bottom lip and scratched the back of his head.

"You're right Jessica I should've said something to you about all this but... I don't know. I... I've been under a lot of stress lately."

Jessica shook her head.

"I can't, I can't do this tonight Greg. Like I told you, I have plans." He didn't say anything in response, Jessica could tell that he was not used to her telling him no.

She wasn't begging for him to take her clothes off, or kiss her, or touch her in those places that only he knew how to make come alive. Jessica wanted the chance not to cave into this man who didn't deserve it. He let go of the doorknob and nodded his head.

"Okay, I will respect that." She tried to shut the door, but he held it. Jessica took a deep breath.

"What, Greg?"

CHAPTER 12

"Call me when you get some free time." She nodded her head.

"I'm serious, Jessica. Call me." She closed the door and reveled in her win over the man she's always allowed to win every time.

Two days later Jessica got a call from Greg, "I need to talk to you, can you please come by my house?"

"I have something to do at the moment. But I can drop by when I'm done." Jessica said.

"Ok, that will be fine." Greg said.

Later that night Jessica went to see Greg. As they talked and laid things on the table, Greg thought it was time to explain to

Jessica why he could not give his all to her at the time.

"Jessica, you know that I love you and care for you, right?"

"Yes, I feel that you love me in your own way and care for me."

"I have been thinking lately, the reason that I don't come around like you want me to is because I don't want to hurt you unnecessarily, and I don't want to wear out my welcome."

"But..." Jessica tried to interrupt.

"Jessica, I feel like I might be on the rebound from my previous relationship that I was in for over thirteen years.
And I think I still have feelings for her.
But I can't get you out of my head or my heart."

"Wow!" That was a punch in the stomach for Jessica.

"I was not expecting to hear you say that to me, whatsoever. So, do you even want to be with me Greg? Or is this just your way of getting out before you are too invested in me and my feelings? Or is this your way of letting me down easy so that you can continue on with the woman I saw you with?"

Greg had no response to what Jessica had asked him. All he could do was sit there and say nothing because he knew that deep down that she was right. He was not ready for Jessica. For what she needed him to be.

He was afraid that he would fuck things up like he did so many years ago with her. And he just could not take the chance to hurt her like that again... Even if he did still have feelings for the other woman, he was in love with Jessica.

Little did Greg know that by him sitting there with nothing to say to Jessica he was breaking her heart all over again, he had no clue that she would do anything for him just to have him in her life.

"Do you want me to wait for you Greg? Do you want me to be here for you while you work out what you need to work out so that we can be together?"

"Jessica, I could never ask you to wait for me. Because what if things don't work out the way that we want them to? I would not feel right knowing that you put your life on hold for me, and then we are not together."

"Greg if I leave right now there is no going back. There will be no waiting for you, no coming back into my life, none of that. So please answer my question, do you want me to wait for you?"

"No, Jessica, I don't want you to wait for me. Because it is not right, and it would be selfish on my part to ask you to do that."

"Okay. Greg as you wish."

Jessica got up kissed Greg one last time and walked out the door; she got into her car and cried all the way home. She knew that the love of her life was gone, and that no matter how much she loved him she could not make him stay. She could not make him love her the way that she loved him. In such a short period Greg had managed to tear down the walls that she had perfectly built around her heart. Only to break her heart like no other.
Jessica couldn't get him out of her head, she thought about him at work. Jessica was mad at him for allowing her to fall for him, but she was madder at herself for letting him do her the way he did and actually loving it.

It was time for Jessica to move on and try to live her life for her and no one else.

Jessica did everything she could to get over Greg. It had been weeks since he told her that he didn't want her to wait for him. Jessica was not one to sit around and feel sorry for herself, so she got up and decided to go out and really put forth an effort to get over Greg.

She spent more time with her son Jaden, put in more hours at work, she even went out on dates with other men, until she no longer thought about him as much. Her divorce had finally been finalized and she was not ready to get back out there and date.

She had finally put Greg to the back of her mind to concentrate on her newly opened bakery. One Thursday, in the middle of December while at work Jessica got a call from one of her girlfriends, Leaha who was a nurse for one of the hospitals.

She and Leaha rarely get a chance to hang out because of their work schedules.

"Hey, Jessica, what are you up to tonight? Want to go get a drink?"

"Hey, Leaha. Girl yes I can use a drink right about now."

"Cool you want to meet up at the 'Three Palms Bar and Grill' around seven o'clock? It's karaoke night."

"Sure, Ok see you there."
Jessica couldn't wait to get off work that night so that she could have some girlfriend time with one of her friends. As Jessica was closing up the shop early that day, a delivery came in just as she was about to lock the doors.

"I have a delivery for Jessica Jackson."

"I'm Jessica Jackson."

"Please sign here for me, please." The delivery guy said.

"Thank you; you have a nice day ma'am."
Jessica was surprised to see a box of her favorite Chocolates and her favorite flowers. Now who sent me this? She wondered to herself. There was a card with it. She read the card "Dear Jessica I'm sorry for how I treated you, can you please forgive me. Love Greg." Jessica took the flowers and candy and tossed them in the trash, he was not gonna do this to me again she thought. Locking the door Jessica, walked to her car and drove home thinking about what she was going to wear that night.

As Jessica parked in her driveway, her neighbor and his usual crowd of friends was out front on his porch. It never fails one of them always tries to come up... Putting on her don't talk to me face Jessica got out the car and went inside. And just as she was opening up her door, her neighbor's friend comes up like clockwork, "hey Ms. Jessica how was work today? You look tired."

Shaking my head, "I am tired today, so if you don't mind..."

"Oh, oh ok, I was just wondering if we could get together one night, and I can take you out for dinner and a drink."

Jessica rolled her eyes, "I'm sorry but I'm just not interested in doing that with anybody at the moment. But thank you for asking." Walking inside and slamming the door. Checking her phone messages, the one person that she did not expect to hear from was on her answering machine.

"Hello, Jessica how have you been? I have been thinking about you. I hope you got the candy and flowers I sent to you. I know that things didn't go very well between us the last time we talked, and I was hoping that I could come over and talk to you. Well let me know when you get in."

"Damn! Damn! Damn!" She said as she walked to her room to get ready to take a shower before going out with her girl tonight. Why does he continue to do this to me, and why do I let it happen? While in the shower, Jessica starts to think about Greg and the way he made her feel, just thinking about him gets her pussy wet. I know I never should've loved him she thought to herself.

Damn! It's been so long since Greg has touched me and caressed me! As Jessica, began to touch herself and wish that it was Greg's hands on her body, inside her, and tasting her juices as they flowed down her legs. Jessica felt the hot water running all over her body as she masturbated in the shower, with tears running down her face and mixing with the water, she hated loving a man that didn't love her back. As her body trembled from her orgasm, she wished that Greg was here to finish the job for her, because she was just not satisfied from masturbating, it only made matters worse to her...

I hate being horny and lonely at the same damn time. She thought as she got out the shower and prepared herself to finish things off with her bullet. As Jessica was getting situated on her bed, her doorbell rings...

"What the fuck!" She said as she got up and put on some sweatpants and a shirt, to answer the door.

Chapter 13

Jessica was ready to scream at whomever was at her door; for interrupting what she was trying to do, she marched to the door. Snatching open the door, Jessica was not prepared to see Greg standing outside her door. Trying to shut the door in his face because at that moment she was way too horny and emotional to let him in.

Because she knew what would come next. It's a good thing she had locked her screen door when she got home.

"Jessica I just need to talk to you for a moment, please."

"What do you want, Greg?" Greg tried to plead his case and apologize for hurting her. But Jessica was not trying to hear it this time. I couldn't do it this time; I just couldn't let him touch me in the state I was in. Greg reached out to try to open the screen door, but it was locked.

"Greg, what do you want?" She asked him again.

"You are so beautiful Jessica; do you know that?"

"No, I'm not, but thank you for saying so."

"Jessica..." He said.

"Please let me in Jessica I miss you." While in the back of her head she thought that this crazy love cycle was about to start all over again.

"No, Greg I can't do that, I can't keep playing this game with you."

"I'm not playing a game; I want you Jessica. He said.

"I was in the middle of something when you rang my doorbell." She said with a sigh.

"Is that right?" "Can I have just a little taste baby? Please."

"No, Greg you can't have a taste. Not this time." She said...

"Are you sure about that, Jessica?" He asked.

"Greg, please we can't do this, you know we can't do this."

"Why not, Jessica?"

"Because you only come around when you want some pussy, not because you want to be with me."

Greg leaned forward and placed his head on the screen door, "Jessica please baby, let me in."

She knew that she had to get ready to go meet her friend for drinks.

"Greg, I have somewhere to be in an hour. So, we can't finish this right now."

"I don't think so." Greg said, you have me hard as a rock and you think I'm gonna leave without tasting you?"

"But I have a date with my friend tonight. I was not expecting you to show up.

"Jessica, call him up and tell him you are not coming."

"Who said it was a guy I was meeting?"

"I don't care who it is, call them, I told you that this is my pussy, and no one is getting this but me. Now call whoever you were meeting tonight and tell them you can't make it."

Jessica knew that if she didn't call her friend, Leaha that Greg was gonna stay there no matter what and deep down inside she knew that this was what she wanted him to do. But she felt bad for wanting to stand her friend up because they really didn't get to see each other regularly.

This was the kind of control Greg had over Jessica, he could make her do things that she would not normally do when it came to other men, or other people. She didn't understand it.

Jessica called Leaha.

"Hey, girl I won't be able to make it tonight something came up. But we will get together soon, I promise."

"Honey, I was gonna call you myself and let you know that I wasn't gonna make it myself, hubby got off work early and he wanted to do something tonight. So, I guess we will try this again another time." Leaha said laughing on the phone.

"Well see you soon, love you."

"Okay, love you too, and you guys have fun, tell Charles I said hello. Bye."

Jessica never understood how this particular man could have so much sexual control over her. He was not her first lover by far, because she had been married and the sex was nothing compared to what she shared with Greg, even twenty years ago he had this same control over her. It was like he knew what she wanted and needed before she did. He knew how to make her feel special when no one else could.

He knew how to make her laugh when she was down. He was the type of man that she needed and wanted in her life. So, she thought. Jessica gave in and opened the door, knowing that she shouldn't. He put his hands in her hair and gently pulled her head back and kissed her softly on the lips. They made love for the better part of the night before they both dozed off into a sound sleep.

CHAPTER 14

Greg woke the next morning with Jessica sleeping on his chest. The feelings that he were having about her were the same feelings that he had so long ago for her. But he was just too afraid of hurting her again. He knew that he loved this woman with his heart and soul, and he knew that he did not want to be without her in his life, not for another twenty years. But he just didn't know how to make things work out the way that he wanted them too. He wanted to marry this woman and make her happy because that is what she deserved in her life some peace and happiness. He knew that somehow; he was going to do the right thing by Jessica. The problem was will he be able to do it before he sent her running into someone else's arms. Jessica was the missing piece of his heart, she made him happy in ways that other women did not. If she only knew how much he loved her then maybe she could understand that everything that he do is for them in the long run. The long hours at work and not being able to spend time with her the way that she wanted him too.

Greg got up out the bed and went into the kitchen to fix breakfast for him and Jessica, he loved doing these kinds of things for her, only because he knew that she deserved to be spoiled, and cherished and treated like a queen. And Jessica always appreciates the simple things that he does for her. Greg ran his large hands down the back of his head, "man this woman has me hook-line-and-sinker, and she doesn't even know it." He said in a whisper to himself. Greg prepared a breakfast of scrambled eggs, with mushrooms, green peppers, onions and cheese, some turkey bacon, grapefruit, strawberries and oranges and a glass of orange juice.

When everything was done, he walked back into Jessica's room and kissed her awake.

"Jessica, baby get up and eat while it's still hot."

"Mmmm, ok."

Jessica got up went into the kitchen to find that Greg had cooked her breakfast and had the table set for two. With a smile on her face Jessica reached up and gave Greg a hug and a kiss.

"Thank you, Greg, you didn't have to do this, but thank you."

"You are more than welcome, beautiful." Knowing that Jessica had to go to work as did he, Greg just wasn't ready to leave yet.

Knowing that she would love to just sit at home and lounge around all day with Greg, Jessica knew that she had a business to run, and that it wasn't gonna open up by itself. One of the things that Jessica loved to do with Greg was taking a shower together, it was when they laughed and joked with each other. It was when he would watch her in the shower before he would join her, that she could see his true feelings for her in his eyes, but just as quick as it was there it was gone. It was like he didn't want her to know how he really felt, like he was protecting himself from heartache and pain, as if Jessica would hurt him.

After their shower Jessica was feeling down because she knew that this was the last time that she would see Greg.

"Greg can we talk before you leave. Please?"

"Sure, what's on your mind," he asked as he leaned in to kiss her. Jessica pulled back from him she did not want him to touch her because she would not be able to tell him what was going through her head.

"I don't want you to come back over anymore after today..."

"what do you mean by that?" He asked interrupting her.

"Because I'm tired of this emotional rollercoaster you have me on. I'm tired of you using me for sex when you get horny, I'm tired of it all. I want to be with someone who wants to be with me and only me, you said yourself that you are not ready for that..."

"Jessica, I don't want to lose you, I want you I really do."

"No, you don't you want sex from me and that's it. So please leave and don't come back. Please Greg. You just can't keep running back to me with your baby, baby please. You had your chance, and you threw it away." She told him.

He lowered his eyes with a sadness she couldn't see, as he left her house her heart was breaking in two as well.

Greg had gradually turned her into his late night and daytime fix, and she didn't know how to break free from that cycle. He dominated her mind, body, and her soul at times. He would call her, she would resist for a while, but by the end of the conversation he was telling her he was on his way over. She noticed that she had never been invited over to his house to spend the night, and that had her always wondering why. She never should've loved him, she thought as she shook her head at the thoughts she was having. It's time for me to move on because this pain is too much for me to continue on down this path.

Plus, I need a vacation, it's been a year since my trip to North Carolina, maybe I will be able to get Greg off my mind and out of my heart for good.

Jessica's cousins were all going on a family cruise in August, she wanted to go, but hated going on vacation with her cousins because all of them were coupled off, even her sister had a man to take with her. And Jessica was the only one flying solo again. Oh, she had someone to ask, but he always had an excuse as to why he couldn't go or participate in something. That made Jessica think and feel like she was just someone he wanted to fuck whenever he needed a release.

But deep down she knew that's all it really was, and that's why she needed to get away from him.

A week later on Friday morning Lynne called Jessica at the shop.

"Are you coming with us on the cruise next month, Jessica?"

"I want to come but, I don't want to be the odd man out again, I hate seeing all you guys all lovey-dovey and shit. And I don't have anyone to be that way with."

"Why don't you ask Greg or see if your friend Winston wants to come with you? Plus, Daisha is going, and she's not bringing her man. Y'all can stay in the same room together, and just split the cost of the room."

"I don't know yet I will let you know next week." That weekend her son Jaden decided to tell her that he wanted to go live with his dad permanently.

"Mom I know you are gonna be upset, but I want to go stay with dad."

"Jaden, you are old enough to make that decision, but I am a little hurt by your decision. I love you and honestly, it's time that you spent more time with your dad. You are sixteen and there are things that I can't show you or teach you that he can." Jessica said to him. Jaden hugged his mom, "I love you mom, you are the best ever."
She smiled at her son as tears slipped from the corners of her eyes, he is growing up so fast she thought to herself.

That following Monday Jessica had, had a long day at the shop and by closing time she had made up her mind to go with her cousins on the cruise. After she got settled at home got dinner fixed and spent time with Jaden before he was to leave to go live with his dad it was a good thing that Jaden was always with his dad whenever Greg came around because she wouldn't know how to explain that to Jaden.

Lying in bed Jessica let the tears fall for all that she had lost in the past year, but she felt it was time for her, time for her to live her life for herself now.

She called her sister Lynne and told her that she would go on the cruise with them. She also told her sister about her and Greg breaking up and how he didn't want to commit to being in a relationship with her.

"Well Jessica you deserve better from any man and maybe it's time for you to step outside the box and meet new people and stop going back to the same lame ass men that you use to date in your past. Because they were in your past for a reason." Lynne told her.

"Maybe you are right sis, maybe it is time for me to get over Brandon and Greg."

For the next several weeks Jessica prepared herself for the cruise with her family, and for once she didn't have Greg on her mind, but it also helped because he didn't come around or call.

She was ready for her vacation cruise, on the Vision Of The Sea, and the itinerary for their seven-day Western Caribbean cruise was lovely.

They would depart from Tampa Florida, dock at Key, West Florida. Then on to Belize City, Belize, then Puerto Costa Maya Mexico, then on to Cozumel, Mexico, then back to Tampa. Jessica couldn't wait to see her cousins and spend some much-needed time in the sun and relax and catch up on some reading, she got her a few new books to take with her. One called Pink Moscato Diaries, and His Soul Mate: Loving Lexie. She had her bags already packed and ready to go. She even went out and bought her a new swimsuit.

CHAPTER 15

CRUISE Day: AUGUST 10, 2013

Today is the family vacation, and Jessica was glad she decided to go along. She planned to relax and enjoy herself.

After their overnight stay at the Holiday Express in Tampa Florida, the family was transported to the cruise-ship.

Jessica and Daisha were in a Royal family Suite on deck nine, that featured two bedrooms, a living area with a sleep sofa, dining room and entertainment center, and two bathrooms.

Lynne, Derrick, Jonathan, and his wife Brandy were also in a Royal Family Suite. All the other family members were in Staterooms along the ninth and tenth floors. Jessica and her cousin Daisha were waiting on the elevator to take them to their floor. When the doors opened, Jessica was struck speechless by the fine brotha standing inside the elevator. He was medium build, with eyes that looked like he was Asian. With a chocolate brown skin complexion with a fade and a wide smile, he took her breath away.

"Damn." she said under her breath. As they got on the elevator and rode it up to the ninth floor.

As the doors opened on their floor Jessica and Daisha got off and so did Mr. Sexy. Jessica noticed that his suite was four doors down from theirs as she walked into their suite, she looked back only to see Mr. sexy looking at her as well. In the suite Jessica asked," did you see him Daisha? He was cute girl."

"See who?' Daisha asked.

"The hottie on the elevator," "oh no, Jessica,
I was busy texting my boyfriend."

"Daisha girl he was too cute with his sexy ass. I think I may just enjoy myself after all."

After putting away their clothes and getting situated in their suite, Jessica decided to check out the ship, and see what her brother and sister were doing, before the emergency drill got started.
She walked out of the suite and bumped into something solid and muscular.

"I'm so sorry," she murmured, as she looked up, Jessica tried to act normal when she noticed that it was Mr. sexy from the elevator, standing outside her suite.

"No problem at all," he said. With a smile that made her all-warm inside. As their eyes met and held, damn he is sexy as hell... Those sexy slanted eyes and full juicy lips... Ooh and his big strong arms... Jessica shook her head to clear away the lustful thoughts before she accidently verbalized what she was thinking.

She cleared her throat.

"Hi, my name is Jean-Jacques Agwé" he told her, holding out his hand.

"It seems that we are going to be neighbors for the next few days." Smiling, she shook his hand.

"I'm Jessica Jackson. It's nice to meet you, Jean."

"I'm in the suite four doors down," he said pointing towards his suite.

Lord, you are really testing me, by putting this sexy hunk of a man down the hall from me, with his sexy accent. If my cousin was not in the same suite with me...

Jessica started laughing, then said "I'm so sorry. I'm a little nervous." She was not going to tell him what she was really thinking.

"It is fine, I love to laugh as well."

"Well, I hope to see you around," Jessica said, then groaned, Jessica hoped she didn't sound like she was trying to come onto him.

"I hope to see you around also," Jean-Jacques replied. He gave her one last look of admiration before she walked away. This trip is starting off great already, she decided with a smile.

Jean-Jacques loved the sound of her laughter. He thought to himself, so far so good. As he watched Jessica walk down the hallway away from her suite. He remembered that she was with another woman on the elevator earlier, he wondered if she was sailing with friends or family. Jean-Jacques also noticed that she wore no wedding ring on her ring finger, but he

wasn't going to assume she was single.
However, Jean-Jacques was going to find out
the next chance he got. He was certain that
he would be sure to run into Jessica on
several occasions throughout the next seven
days. Jean-Jacques wasn't going to come on
this cruise at first, but now he's glad that he
decided to come. Jean-Jacques returned to
his suite after a short stroll on the upper
deck and looking for the gym. He wanted to
take a quick nap before he went down to the
pool for a swim. He stifled a yawn as he
remembered the emergency drill that was
required for them to attend. Jean-Jacques
took out some business papers to go over
until it was time for the drill. His mind kept
drifting back to Jessica. He would really like
to have another conversation with her.
Jean-Jacques didn't know what it was, but
there was something special about her. After
the drill Jean-Jacques took a quick nap
before heading out to the pool area for some
rest and relaxation.

"Jessica, you look cute, so stop worrying,"
Lynne said, leaning against the rail.

"Let's go, everyone is at the pool waiting
for us."

Jessica had on her new two-piece navy blue and white bathing suit with matching see through cover up and some navy and white slip-on's.

As they stepped outside, she took in her surroundings. It was just amazing how the sun seemed to wash over the ocean in brilliant colors.

"Damn, Jessica you got all the guys staring at you already, and we just got out here."

Laughing, Jessica shook her head, "girl you crazy. You know they ain't looking at me, they might be looking at you."

"No, honey they're looking at you. Oh, my goodness, Jessica look at him. He is staring you down girl, and he's cute." Shading her eyes from the sun, Jessica followed Lynne's gaze. Standing close by the bar was a tall slender guy with short hair, and brown skin that glistened in the August sun. His slim frame was well defined with muscles in all the right places. His swim trunks hung low on his hips. The effect was breathtaking, way to sexual. There wasn't any fat on Jean's body, and the way his muscles moved in all the right places. Jessica's skin began to tingle as she felt herself get wet.

Get ahold of yourself, she told herself.

"That's the guy I was telling you about."

"The one you met in the hallway?" With a smile on her face, Lynne waved at him.

"What are you doing?" Jessica asked.

"I'm getting his attention for you." Lynne said laughing. Jean-Jacques waved back at them. Jessica ran her fingers through her shoulder-length curly hair. The thought of running into Jean-Jacques again made her nervous and excited at the same time.

"Hello, ladies," Jean-Jacques said as they got closer. His deep sexy voice, with his foreign accent greeted them as they walked over to him.

"Would you like to join us? Lynne asked, we're going to be hanging out around the pool with our family. Oh, are you with someone, I'm sorry?" Jessica, didn't realize she was holding her breath, waiting for his response. She didn't see him with anyone, but that didn't mean he was on vacation by himself.

"I'm here by my lonesome, I'm afraid." Jessica just loved to hear him speak, it was like melted candle wax oozing down her body and making her wet.

"What about you Jessica? Are you traveling with anyone?"

"No, besides my family I'm here solo." He had the most sexist voice she had ever heard and some pretty brown eyes, the way they slanted at the corners. Those eyes kept looking at her left hand.

"I take it you're not married, then?" Jessica smiled, "No I don't have a husband at the moment."

"I'm glad to hear."

"Really, now?" Jessica asked.

"Well on that note, I think I will go find Derrick, And see if Matthew and Torrie are coming down. You two just keep on chatting." Lynne said as she winked at Jessica and walked away.

"I love your accent, where are you from?" Jean-Jacques smiled at Jessica with his wide lips and beautiful white teeth.

"I'm from Haiti. I am on holiday for the next seven days." He replied. Jessica smiled, as she looked at Jean, "welcome to America, I hope you enjoy your visit."

Jean's dark brown eyes, stared at Jessica, he didn't tell her that he now lived in America, but was on holiday from his job.

"I was hoping to bump into you again."

"Really? Why is that?"
Jean-Jacques tilted his head slightly to the side.

"Jessica, you are very beautiful, and I find you very intriguing. I would like to know more about you."
Jessica stared into his eyes to see if he was trying to run some kind of game, but they seemed to be sincere. As Jessica relaxed Jean-Jacques found two empty lounge chairs for them to sit in and continue on with their conversation. More of Jessica's family began to drift down to the pool area. Jonathan Jessica and Lynne's brother came and introduced himself to Jean, while they were talking. Brandy his wife, and Shantel their cousin came to sit down beside Jessica.

"I see you Jessica" Shantel said in a whisper.

"Yeah, who's the hottie?" Brandy asked, leaning over Shantel.

"Are you serious?" Daisha said as she came and sat down next to Brandy.

"He ain't all that." Shantel and Brandy both looked at her and said, "you must be blind, if you can't see that he is fine."
Jonathan walked around and grabbed Brandy's hand, "let's get in the pool."

"You have a big family," he said as Shantel and Daisha got up to follow Jonathon and his wife to the pool.
Shantel turned back around "oh yeah, Matt and Torrie said that they will meet us at dinner, the twins were being fussy, so they weren't coming down Amber and Jason said they'll be down soon."

Jessica laughed, "you haven't seen them all, some are still in their suites and the other half couldn't make it on this trip. His eyes widened in surprise at what she had just told him. Jessica chuckled at his surprised look, "It's a bunch of us on the cruise."

"Is this some kind of family reunion?" She nodded, "sort of. We try to get together a few times a year. It's mostly the cousins and my siblings that go on vacations together."

"It looks like you guys are pretty close."

"Yeah, we are, we pretty much grew up together."

"Jean-Jacques you should join us, later for dinner," Jonathan said as he climbed out the pool.

"We have dinner reservations at the Chops Grille."

"Sure, I'd love to," he answered. As Jessica stood up, she said, "I don't know about you, but I'm getting in the pool."

CHAPTER 16

Jean-Jacques put his hand to his eyes to shade them from the sun, "well I guess I will join you in the pool."

Lynne and Brandy smiled in amusement as they watch Jessica walk towards them with Jean.

They stopped at the pool and Jessica stepped in, wading towards Lynne and Brandy. Jean-Jacques's dove into the water near her, Jessica felt the water move as he dove in. She pushed her hair out of her face and tried to move away as he splashed her with water playfully.

"Oh, you want to play, two can play at this game." She said laughing as she splashed him back with water. After playing in the water with Jessica like kids, Jean-Jacques climbed out to get them something to drink. Amber and Jason joined them in the pool.

"I see you sis, looks like y'all are getting along well with each other." Lynne whispered in Jessica's ear.

"Yes, we are," she whispered back.

"Who is the cutie with Jessie?" Amber asked Lynne.

"That's Jean, they met on the elevator earlier Shantel" said with a grin.

"What happened to Greg?
I thought they were going out." Amber replied.

"Girl, she finally left him alone, he was playing too many games."
Lynne told the group. Amber looked over at Jason with a scowl on her face, "your friend hurt my cousin again and you didn't tell me." Jason looked at her and shrugged his shoulders, "babe Greg didn't tell me that they were no longer together, I swear." He said with his hands in the air.

Lynne, Shantel, Brandy and Daisha all started getting out the pool.

"We're going to take a nap and check on the kids before dinner," Shantel said as they all left the pool.

"Your, cousins they are leaving?" Jean-Jacques asked, when he walked back with their drinks. She nodded, as she told him, that they all went to take a nap before dinner. Jean-Jacques smiled to himself, as Jessica got out to drink her drink that he had gotten for her. Jessie introduced him to her cousin Amber and her boyfriend Jason, they talked for a few more minutes, before they to left the pool. He just couldn't get over how many of her family members were on the ship, and he liked the fact that they were all close. Jean-Jacques couldn't take his eyes off her. He thought of her smooth caramel complexion, light hazel eyes and the way her hair curled up when wet.

She was an extremely beautiful woman. She wasn't too thin, or too heavy, she was curvy and thick in all the right places. Just the way he liked. Jessica tapped him on the shoulder, and asked,

"where were you? What were you thinking about so hard?"

Jean-Jacques snapped out of his reverie. Jean-Jacques confessed, "I was actually thinking about you."

Laughing, she playfully tapped him on the arm.

"You don't quit, do you?"

"I am serious, I was thinking about you." Jessica looked down and shook her head.

"Please, let's not get to serious about anything. We're on vacation; let's just enjoy our time together. We are here to have fun." Jean-Jacques thought Jessica looked sad when she'd said that, but her expression quickly changed. He told himself that maybe it was his imagination.

DAY TWO:
PORT OF CALL, KEY WEST, FLORIDA.

They spent the day together looking
through shops and having lunch, they met
back up with her family on the ship around
two-thirty, to go to one of the shows on the
ship before dinner. Jessica and Jean-Jacques
got to know more about each other and was
enjoying each other's time and company
while on the ship. They agreed to share their
cruise with one another, being that they
were both sailing alone without a significant
other.
Jessica's family and Jean-Jacques had
dinner at the Chef's table with a five-course
gourmet meal and wine tasting.
Later they walked the deck looking out at
the moon-light and looking out over the sea.

Lynne and Derrick came out, to join them and they enjoyed friendly conversation, Jean-Jacques told them about his country and how things were different there, then they are here in the U.S. Jessica's sister liked Jean-Jacques and let her know it.

"I think he's nice Jessica, he seems to really like you
Jessie."

Lynne said quietly to Jessica while the men were talking about sports.

"Yes, he does, but I didn't come on this cruise to meet a guy let alone hook up with one." Lynne shook her head at her sister because she just didn't get it, "no one said that you had to hook up with him, but damn let yourself have fun once in a while, let your hair down and live life, that's all I'm saying."

Jessica looked at her sister and smiled,

"you are right sis, it's time to start living my life the way I want and stop moping around over a man, that is not thinking about me."

Jessica hugged her sister, and asked Jean-Jacques if he was ready to go get a nightcap before turning in for the night.

DAY THREE: AT SEA

Jessica got up early to hit the gym and get her workout in before she got her day started, the family had agreed to meet for breakfast later, and do some on board rock climbing. Jessica, Lynne, Brandy, Daisha, Shantel, Amber and Torrie their cousin Matthew's wife, all had a scheduled appointment at the day spa, for full body massages while Jonathan, Derrick, Matthew, Jordan, Jason, and Jean, and some of their other cousins went to the casino.

Torrie and Brandy took their little ones to the kids play center before meeting up at the day spa.

"Jessica, I see that you are enjoying your vacation," Brandy said.

"Yeah, I see you have an admirer also tagging around with you." Torrie added with a smile on her face, Torrie was a black girl in a white girl's body, She was part of the family and we didn't see her as anything but that.

"It's nice to see you relaxing and smiling more," Lynne said, and the other ladies agreed with her. They enjoyed their spa day treatments, without the men.

"I hope the guys aren't giving Jean-Jacques the third-degree," Brandy said with a loud laugh.

"So, Jean, man I see you like my sister, Jessie." Jonathan said.

"Yes, she is a very beautiful woman, and I like her joy for life."

"So, are you in the US to find a wife or something?" Matthew asked with a smile on his lips. Jean-Jacques laughed, "no I am US citizen and no I'm not looking for an American wife, but if I happen to find one that would be nice too."

"So, what do you do for a living Jean?" Jonathan asked.

"I own several restaurants around the world," he said with a smile on his face. They all looked at each other and started laughing."

"You and Jessie will get along just fine because she owns a bakery called Jessica's Sweet Treats. You should look her up sometime." Jonathan said.

They all sat around the casino bar for a while longer before heading back to their rooms to shower and change before meeting the others in the lobby for dinner at the Aquarius Dining Room, on one of the upper decks.

Chapter 17

DAY Four: BELIZE CITY, BELIZE
THE FORMER CAPITAL, BELIZE CITY
IS THE GATEWAY TO AN ARRAY OF
ADVENTURES.

They docked in Belize City, Belize.
Everyone was excited to see the city, they all
met in the lobby with cameras in hand·
    As they toured the city, Jessica took
photos of the historic Mayans Mountains, this
is said to be the gateway to an array of
adventures. They walked through the
rainforest and toured the Mayan ruins. Jean-
Jacques walked behind Jessica taking
pictures with his camera.

"Would you be interested in going to El Castillo?" Jean-Jacques asked Jessica.

"Sure, let's check it out," she relied. Jean-Jacques pulled Jessica close to him. When he put his arm around her Jessica felt like she'd come home. She felt safe with him. For the first time Jessica didn't have Greg on her mind, but she wished that he was the one here sharing this cruise with her. But he had been sending her so many mixed signals lately.

Jessica put on a smile and thought why worry about a man that is not worried about her. Hours into their tour of the city, Jessica received a text from Lynne, "my sister and cousins are going into the city for lunch and shopping. They seem to have had enough of the history lesson." Jessica told Jean.

"Would you like to go with them?" Jean-Jacques asked.

Jessica shook her head, placed her hands on her hips, "are you saying that because I'm a woman, that I want to spend my time shopping?" Jean-Jacques laughed and held up his hands in defense. "No, No, No I'm not saying that. I just know that you are on holiday with you family, and I thought you might want to spend some time with them."

"No, we are going to see El Castillo," Jessica stated in a tone that meant no argument. "I will catch up with them later on the beach."

She was enjoying her time with Jean. She could see her family anytime. After touring El Castillo and the mountains, they visited the tiny city, they went to do the cave-and-river tubing. Later they grabbed a bite to eat, then strolled down along the Caribbean coastline towards the beach where her family were to meet up.

"Belize is so beautiful," Jessica whispered. Jean-Jacques agreed as he finished off his water. Jessica spotted her family down on the beach. She looked at her watch, "I guess I better head that way for some family time. What are you going to do?" She prayed that he would like to join her.

"I didn't have any plans. If it's okay with you, I would like to spend the rest of my day with you."

Jessica smiled. "I'm really glad you said that. Did you bring your swimsuit?" Jean-

Jacques nodded, "it's in my backpack. I'm always prepared." Jean-Jacques was almost too perfect, but she had only known him for a couple of days.

She smiled as she thought about all she knew about him. She knew that he was from Haiti, and that he moved to the United States about five years ago for his job, and that he now lives in Miami Florida. She wondered if they would stay in touch after the cruise was over, she hoped they would.

Jean-Jacques caught her staring at him more than once, and he just smiled at her. He was a very sexy man, something about him drew her to him and made her want more than just a friendship with him.

Shantel, Lynne, Brandy and Torrie all stood by Jessica and watched her as she watched Jean-Jacques interacting with her brother and male cousins.

"It seems like you two hitting it off," Lynne whispered close to her ear.

"Yes, we are having a good time, I have no expectations beyond this trip. We are enjoying ourselves together, and it's not like he is looking for a relationship, or anything."

"Would you be open to it if he was looking for one?" Shantel asked. Jessica grinned, "I'll take it one day at a time."

By two-o'clock Jean-Jacques yawned, and stretched, "I think I'm gonna head back to the ship and take a nap," Jessica stood up as he brushed sand from his swim trunks.

"I'll see you all later tonight." Jessica gave him a hug, "I'll see you later," she said. As Jean-Jacques walked away Daisha had something to say as usual, "don't get too attached to him," she said.

"Jessica is enjoying herself, let her. You should try doing the same thing." Lynne interjected.

"Daisha, I'm just having fun with a very nice and handsome man. I have no illusions about anything, beyond this crise. I'm here to enjoy myself and have a good time while on vacation. Why don't you try it yourself?" Jessica said as she picked up her things and headed back to the ship.

"See Daisha you just don't know how to stop, do you?" Shantel said. Daisha picked up her bag and walked away shaking her head. Everyone gathered up their things and started back towards the ship, the relaxing mood had been broken. Back in their suite,

Jessica went to her room, to change and shower. Daisha knocked on her door. "Jessica, I'm sorry for what I said earlier, I just don't want you to get hurt like you did before."

"Jean-Jacques and I are having a good time together; I enjoy his company." Jessica walked into the bathroom to take a shower. Afterward she got into bed and fell asleep. Daisha felt bad for what she said to her cousin, but she was just telling the truth how she saw it. Plus, she was in a bad mood because she and her man were going through some things as well. She wanted to tell her cousins that she and had found her boyfriend in bed with another woman before the trip and that's why he was not here with her. But she didn't want them to know that her life wasn't as perfect as she portrayed it to be.

Daisha woke Jessica up just in time to get ready before dinner and for them to meet up with the family. Jessica pulled her shoulder length hair up into an updo with ringlets of curls hanging down to frame her face.

She put on her blue V-neck sundress that touched the floor, with side slits on both sides, that hugged her curvy figure to a tee. She slipped on some matching blue and silver four-inch open toe wedges, and her white gold charm bracelet and matching blue and silver earrings.

She added her favorite perfume Exotic Jasmine by Halle Berry, Looked at herself in the mirror for a final check and was ready to head to dinner.

"You look gorgeous," Daisha told her.

"Girl when Jean-Jacques sees you tonight, you won't be able to get rid of him." Jessica laughed and turned from the mirror to look at Daisha.

"I doubt that." But deep down, she was hoping that her cousin was right, but she knew not to get her hopes up high.

"Daisha, I have a confession to make. You see, the truth is I like Jean, we seem to click. I don't know what it is, but we have a lot in common."

CHAPTER 18

Their family was waiting for them down it the lobby, Jessica spotted Jean-Jacques as they stepped off the elevator. Jean-Jacques placed Jessica's hand in the crook of his arm and led her towards the dining room. He leaned down close to her ear, "you look beautiful, you are a sight to see. Your dress looks good on you." He told her. Jessica smiled, "Thank you." She whispered softly to him.

They all enjoyed dinner and dancing, in the Viking Crown Lounge, after dancing, Torrie, Matthew, Jonathan and Brandy all went to check on their kids, in the nursery.

The next morning Jessica started her day off in the spa and fitness center, like she always did at home, she was determined to

keep her weight on track, She wasn't
expecting to see Jean-Jacques in the gym.

"Hey, Jean." she said when she saw him.

"Hi yourself, you working out today too I
see. We could work out together if you like."
He said.

"Sure, that's fine." Jessica replied. As they
worked out, she enjoyed the time that they
spent together in the gym working out.
She began to think that Greg would never
take the time do something like this with
her. Even when she asked him to. She
cleared her mind, telling herself no more
thinking of Greg on this cruise.
They felt the ship slowing down as it pulled
into port. They had arrived at Puerto Costa,
Maya Mexico. As they walked back to their
suites after their workout, "your brother
Jonathan has invited me to join you all
today. I hope that would be ok with you. I
don't want you to think that I'm trying to
take up all of your time, on your holiday."
Jean-Jacques said to her.

"No, I enjoy your company, and I would
love for you to join us, plus I love to hear
you speak, and I love our conversations that
we have." Jessica laughed.

Jessica and Jean-Jacques agreed to meet in forty-five minutes. They hugged and went to their own suites to get ready for the day. Daisha was coming out of her room when Jessica entered their suite.

"There is so much history here in Puerto Costa, I want to visit the Mayan ruins." Jessica said to Daisha. After a quick shower, Jessica put on a very basic blue-jean romper set with quarter length sleeves and side pockets, and white New Balance tennis shoes. She grabbed her backpack, floppy hat, and sunglasses to protect her from the sun. Everyone met down in the lobby. She spotted Jean-Jacques and couldn't stop smiling because they were similarly dressed. He was wearing a pair of Levi's blue-jean shorts with a white Polo shirt with hat to match, and white Air-Max 97's. Everyone else was dressed in shorts and t-shirts and tennis shoes. That feeling came over Jessica and she knew the truth of her feeling for this man that she had only just met. Jessica was falling in love with Jean. She had fallen for his warm heart and his loving spirit. Something she had never done before. She had some thinking to do, and some decisions to make when she returned home from her cruise.

The group all traveled by coach to the city of Puerto Costa, Maya. This was Jean's first time seeing sparkling sands and turquoise seas.

Jessica and Jean-Jacques experienced this beautiful sight together, for their first time. They toured the pyramid at Chacchoben.

They went to the nearby town of Mahahual, a small fishing village. Jean-Jacques held Jessica's hand while they toured the Mayan ruins in the jungle. They explored the coral reef in the sea.

Jessica was having such a wonderful time with Jean that she didn't want to leave. She smiled up at him, he loved to see her smile. Her smile seemed to always make his heart beat faster.

Jean-Jacques was finding it hard to control his emotions more and more around her. He knew that the feelings he were having were feelings he had not had for a woman in a very long time.

Jean-Jacques bent his head down and kissed Jessica softly on the lips he caught her off guard.

Four hours later they agreed it was time to head back to the ship to get ready for dinner. Back in her suite she found Daisha resting on the sofa and reading a book before dinner.

"I am so glad that I came on this cruise." Jessica stated with a smile on her face. Daisha smiled at her, "Me too. I'm truly having a good time." Daisha said, with a smile.

"I think we should get ready for dinner; the others will be waiting for us down in the lobby area." Daisha agreed.

A few hours later, they were ready to head out.
Jessica was dressed in a wine V-neck, ankle length jumpsuit, with lantern style sleeves, with gold accessories and black wedges. She had her hair pulled up loosely on top of her head with ringlets of hair falling around her face. Daisha had on a black and wine-colored button up dress with gold accents and wine and gold heels.

"You look sexy, Daisha," Jessica said when she saw Daisha coming out her room.

"No, you look fabulous as well." Daisha told her. They left the suite and found Jean-

Jacques outside waiting for them, he smiled when he saw the ladies dressed to kill.

"You two look beautiful." He told them as he took Jessica's hand and held it, and took the elevator to deck twelve, to the Izumi Restaurant, where they served Asian dishes, like sushi rolls, sashimi, hot rock Ishiyaki plates and more.

When they arrived some of the family was already seated. Jessica sat next to her brother, Jonathan and his wife Brandy with Jean-Jacques seated across from her.

"I haven't seen much of you Jessica," her brother said. Jessica smiled, "I've been busy." Jessica felt the heat from Jean's stare, she turned to look at him as he gave her a wink. After dinner everyone went their own way to do their own thing with their spouses. Jean-Jacques and Jessica took a walk outside, he held her hand, as they walked and talked about all kinds of things. Jessica closed her eyes and welcomed the night air on her face. Jean-Jacques wrapped his arms around her and pulled her close.

"I'm enjoying spending time with you Jessica." She looked up at him.

"Me too, Jean." Jessica felt the heat of desire wash over her; she was getting wet.

Jean-Jacques turned her to face him, he leaned down and kissed her softly on the lips. Jessica reached up and pulled him closer to her, to deepen their kiss. The night air washed over her and made her tremble. Her senses out of control, she broke their kiss, and placed her head on his chest; She clung to him as she trembled from the heat of their kiss.

Chapter 19

She could feel his manhood start to rise.

"Why you so quiet?" He asked.

"I was thinking that you are a wonderful kisser, and I enjoyed it. And would like to try it again, but I'm afraid that if we do, I may want to it further than just a kiss."

"Your honesty, amazes me Jessica." They walked and talked, learning new things about each other, telling funny stories about themselves. Jean-Jacques just loved the way her face lit up when she talked about her family and children. It made him happy to see her happy because he could tell that

145

somewhere in her life, she has a lot of sadness. They ran into Lynne and Derrick while walking. Jean-Jacques and Derrick shook hands, while Lynne and Jessica hugged, "I see that you and your friend are spending a lot of time together. It's nice to see you smiling again." Jessica looked over at Jean-Jacques and smiled, "yes, it feels good to smile again."

Jean-Jacques wanted to take Jessica back to his suite and make love to her. His body was on fire for this woman, she made his dick hard just thinking about her. She had him so heated that he had to take several cold showers while on the cruise. Jean-Jacques and Jessica said goodbye to her sister and Derrick.

They walked hand in hand, "would you like to come back to my room for a night cap, and sit out on the balcony and look out to sea?" Jean-Jacques asked Jessica.

"Sure, why not." She said with a smile. They headed back to his suite. He turned to look at Jessica and smiled at her. He let her enter his suite first, he followed and turned on the lights. Jean-Jacques poured them both a glass of wine and they went and sat on the balcony of his suite.

They sat in silence just enjoying the view. Jean-Jacques thought about the feelings he was having for Jessica. To him she was almost perfect. She had some of the qualities he wanted in a woman, she was intelligent, honest and most of all she was beautiful. If his mother was still living, she would love Jessica, even though she was not of their culture. There was no drama, or secrets' nothing like his first marriage.

Jessica reached over and kissed Jean-Jacques on the cheek, "thank you."

"For what are you thanking me?" He asked.

"For making my vacation the best. And for spending your holiday with me and my family." Jean-Jacques smiled at her and took her hand in his "stay with me tonight, Jessica. I just want to hold you tonight". Jessica, lowered her eyes in thought, she looked at Jean-Jacques and said, "I would like that."

They finished off their wine and retired for the night. That night they made love for the first time. Jessica was amazed at how gentle he was with her during their love making, it was amazing how he loved her, it was like no other. Jessica knew that she would not be the same after this. Jean-Jacques ordered room service for them; he was not ready to let her go. As they lounged in bed, they pulled into port at Cozumel, Mexico. They made love one more time before hitting the shower together.

They planned their day before Jessica left his suite to head to hers to get ready. Jean-Jacques kissed her before she left his room, agreeing that he would stop by her room to get her around ten-thirty, which gave her an hour and thirty minutes to get ready for their day in Cozumel.

Entering her suite, "well, well, well, look what the cat drug in." Her cousin said with a smile on her face. Jessica, laughed.

"Well how was it, spill the beans?" Daisha said flopping down on the sofa in the main area of their suite.

"It was amazing Daisha; he was so gentle and took his time. Girl it took my breath away. He's a good kisser and an amazing lover."

"Well, I'm glad that you are having fun and that you have gotten that asshole off your mind, cause he was just not right for you, Jessica."

Jessica had a sad look in her eyes, "yeah, I know cuz, He was one that I just shouldn't have loved a second time around, or at all for that matter." Jessica said. Jessica got up to get ready for Jean-Jacques to pick her up for the day.

Jean, Jessica, and her family all left the port by coach, agreeing to meet back up in a few hours to catch the coach back to the ship. Jean-Jacques and Jessica went shopping in the town of San Miguel. They toured the botanical gardens. Jean, Jessica walked hand-in-hand as they followed some of the other passengers through the town.

"Have you ever been to Mexico before?" She asked Jean.

"No, this is my first time here."

"Where all have you been?"

"I've been to Canada for a while, before I moved to Florida, I was married before, but it didn't work out. What about you?"

"Well, I have been a few places, being that my dad was in the service. I lived in Florida for a while and North Dakota for a summer.

"Oh, you were close to Canada then." Jessica smiled, "Yes, a long time ago. I now live in Dayton, Ohio. I just came back from a trip to North Carolina, to visit my cousin Amber about a year ago. This cruise here is my first cruise that I have taken with my family." Jessica said.

"My family is still in Haiti, I have three brothers, our mother passed away when I was a boy. I miss Haiti a lot. I will go home to visit them one day." He said with sadness in his eyes. Jessica looked into Jean's eyes, they looked so sad. How she wished that she could take the pain and sadness away. They went to mainland the home of the Tulum, Mayan cliff-side ruins, that overlooked the Caribbean.

Jean, Jessica checked out the underwater world of Chankanaab aboard the Atlantis submarine. They caught up with her family and they all took pictures of each other and together.

Jessica's heart swelled with so much joy and what she felt was love, every time she looked at this beautiful man. Several times Jessica caught him staring at her, she wondered what he was thinking about, but was afraid to ask him. The group enjoyed lunch at one of the local cafes before heading back to the coach, for their return to the ship.

"My family seems to like you," Jessica said.

"Have they been giving you a hard time about me?" She laughed, "no, not really just the normal jokes that they have, but nothing serious. Me and Daisha were the only ones not coupled off, so meeting you has been wonderful for me."

Chapter 20

Jean- Jacques looked at her, "you are so incredibly sexy, Jessica."
She blushed, "thank you, Jean."

"I just love your honesty; it is so refreshing." He said to Jessica.

"It sounds like you've had a bad experience in your past relationship."

"Yes, I found out that my wife was sleeping with two of my friends, during the three and a half years that we were married. I despise a person that lies and keeps secrets." He said. Jessica grew quiet and looked away, she began to bite her bottom lip.

Jean noticed that she had never done that before now.

"What's wrong, Jessica?" She looked sad all of a sudden, and he had no idea why. But he had a feeling it had to do with something or someone back in her hometown, and that is why she was on holiday so soon after just taking a holiday one year ago.

Jean-Jacques knew that he was falling for this woman and he was willing to try to keep her in his life. He just hoped that she felt the same way as he did, and that she could trust him with her heart and her love. They were to go Salsa dancing later that night, but he just wanted to spend some quiet time with her and maybe she would open up and talk to him about why she was so sad and unhappy.

"I hope you don't mind, Jean if we don't go Salsa dancing tonight, I don't feel up to it."

Jean-Jacques took her hands in his, her touch sending tremors through his body.

"No, baby I don't mind if we don't go, we can take in a movie on deck nine. And just chill for the night."

Jean walked her back to her suite. He pulled her close and kissed her. She looked up at him and agreed to doing the movies instead of going dancing.

"I will be back to get you around seven-thirty that way we can stop at the Wind Jammer Cafe for a bite to eat before the show starts." Jessica went inside and closed the door behind her.

She had the worst feeling ever, she knew that she would have to tell Jean-Jacques about Greg, because she once loved Greg but was just getting over him. Jessica knew that she was ready to settle down, with one person, and someone who loved her.

Jessica tried to take a nap before her date with Jean. She tossed and turned all the while thinking about how she has come to have deep feelings for Jean, but how she still had love for Greg.

She really needed to do some soul searching because she was tired of playing the game that Greg wanted to play. Jessica got up and went to stand out on the balcony to clear her head and think.

Spending time with Jean-Jacques these past few days have been the best for her.

She had developed strong feelings for him, and for a second she allowed herself to think that they might be able to continue seeing each other. But that changed when Jean-Jacques said that he hates secrets. Jessica made up her mind, she was going to tell Jean-Jacques tonight when he picks her up for the movie. Daisha knocked on Jessica's door, "are you coming down for dinner with the family?"

"No, not yet going down with Jean later, right now I just need some time alone for a while." She said.

"Ok sweetie, you sure you're alright?" Daisha asked.

"No, I'm not alright," she replied, "but I will be later." Jean-Jacques picked Jessica up for their date, when he saw her, he knew something wasn't right with her, but didn't know how to bring up the subject. He just hoped and prayed that she would trust him enough to tell him the issue.
Later during dinner, Jean-Jacques held her hand on the table,

"Jessica, *babe mwen konnen yon bagay ki mal, tanpri di kisa li ye,* Jean-Jacques said in Haitian Creole. Jessica looked at him in awe, she had never heard him speak Creole before.

"What did you say, Jean?" *"e mwen renmen nou Jessica, sa fe mwen mal pou mwen we nou tris."*

"I said, babe I know something is wrong, please tell me what it is, and that I love you Jessica, it hurts my heart to see you sad."

Tears slid down her face, and she had no choice but to tell him what was going on. "Jean, I have come to have feelings for you, I didn't come on this cruise to find a man or even have an affair. I came on this vacation to get a man off my mind.

You see while I was in North Carolina I ran into an old love of mine we hooked up and had an affair that left me feeling used and taken advantage of and broken. We hardly ever spent time together, all we ever did was have sex. But I wanted more, even though I am recently divorced, I was still ready to settle down with one man, a man that wanted to be with me and I thought that Greg was that man until he told me that he wasn't ready for what I wanted. And that he was still getting over a relationship that ended."

CHAPTER 21

Jean-Jacques now understood her sadness and vowed to himself that if she agreed to continue to see him that she would never feel used and unappreciated.

"So, I came on this trip to get over him and move on with my life, for my heart's sake. Then I met you and I was torn between my feelings for you and the feelings I had left for Greg." Jessica felt the weight leave her chest and she felt so much better after her confession. Jean-Jacques leaned over the table and kissed her on the lips.

"Let's get out of here," he said. They went back to his suite, and he did things to her that made her forget that another man had ever occupied her mind.

Jean-Jacques made love to Jessica like his life depended on it, he was focused on making her his, because from what she told him about this Greg, he was someone that she never should've loved from the start. They made love in the shower, he turned her towards the shower wall and lifted her left foot up onto the edge of the tub, he carefully crouched down on his knees and kissed her from her ankles all the way to her lower back leaving nothing untouched. He could hear her moaning from the sheer pleasure of his gentle kisses.

He took a rag and soaped it up, washed her all over, and rinsed her off. Jean-Jacques had wanted to do this the first time they made love, but he knew that she wasn't ready for how he could pleasure her at that time. Jean-Jacques turned her around to face him, he caressed her body, loving the way her skin felt beneath his fingertips. He drew one of her breasts into his mouth, sucking her nipple, as he lightly bit it; making her scream his name. Jessica placed her hands on his head and pulled his head closer to her breast. She was so wet and ready to release her juices, but she wanted it to last a little longer. Jessica pushed him gently to the other side of the shower, she placed kisses all over his body, taking time to lick his nipples and gently rub her teeth across his swollen buds, causing him to shudder.

Jessica kissed him on his stomach going lower and lower, until she came to his long hard dick, she stroked it, making him moan with pleasure from her touch. Jean-Jacques was loving her touch on him. She felt him tremble beneath her touch and it made her gain courage to continue with her oral love making. Jean-Jacques felt himself about to explode he gently pulled her up, kissing her passionately on the lips and neck. Jean-Jacques was falling in love with her more and more every minute, that he was with her. He loved touching her and holding her. He just wanted to love her hurt away and show her that love can be forever.

Jean-Jacques picked her up and wrapped her legs around him as he backed her up against the shower wall and made love to her right there in the shower. As the warm water ran down her face, soaking her hair and running down over her breast, she looked so beautiful to him, as he made love to her passionately. Jean-Jacques washed her off once again, then himself. He carried her out the shower and to his bed where they made love all night, falling asleep a little after four in the morning. Jean-Jacques woke up with Jessica in his arms, he smiled to himself, from sheer happiness of finding this amazing woman. Jean-Jacques and Jessica shared breakfast in bed that morning, she had a smile on her face because she felt free to allow this wonderful man into her life. She was falling fast for this man, and she welcomed it.

They showered and dressed. Jean-Jacques walked her to her suite, so that she could change into something comfortable, they were going to take in that movie that they missed the night before and go to the gift shop to purchase more gifts for her family and friends. This was their last day at sea, and he wanted to spend it with just her.

"I can't believe this is our last day of our holiday. The time has flown by." Jean-Jacques said.

"I know, it has been wonderful for me, meeting you was a bonus," Jessica said with a smile and kissed him on the lips. They left the gift shop, with gifts for her family and kids and her staff at her bakery shop. They walked hand in hand, to put the gifts in her room before heading to lunch and the movies.

"What happens between us now that our cruise is almost over?" Jessica asked Jean, over lunch.

"We both live in different places, but I don't see why we can't continue to see each other from time to time.

Unless you are not interested in seeing me again." Jean-Jacques said. Jessica squinted her eyes at him in disbelief because his question kind of caught her off guard, she was not expecting to hear him to say that.

"Of course, I would love to continue seeing you."
Jean-Jacques smiled and picked her up from her seat and hugged her.

"I was hoping you would say that." He confessed, "because I don't want what we have to end."

Jessica smiled at him and kissed him soundly on the lips.

"I don't want it to end either," she said with a big grin on her face.

"I wasn't looking to meet someone like you on this cruise. I wasn't even gonna come, but my sister Lynne and cousins talked me into coming." She said.

"I believe things happen for a reason; we were supposed to meet." Jean said.

"I want and need you so much, I can't think straight."

Jean kissed her, "I want you too," he said softly. They went back to his suite and made love all over again. It was unbelievable, how he made her feel every time they came together. Not only could he get her wet just from his touch, but he also made her wet every time he looked at her or spoke to her in Creole. Jessica couldn't believe that a man could be so gentle yet make her vagina throb so hard.

It really felt right, not like she was trying to convince him to want her or need her. Jean-Jacques made her feel loved and wanted. And he knew how to eat the pussy right, Jessica laughed at her last thoughts, but she was serious all the same. Jessica knew that this would change everything from here on out. She had fallen in love with a man she had just met, and it felt so right.

Jean-Jacques looked over at her, *"Mwen te ka toumante ou chak."* He said in Creole.

"What did you just say?" She asked him.

"I said, I could tease to please you every day."

"Ou se soley mwen ak lalin mwen." He kissed her on the forehead. They showered and Jessica returned to her suite to pack for tomorrow, she was walking on cloud nine, and loving every minute of it. Daisha noticed the change in Jessica the moment she walked through the door. She smiled at her cousin, but didn't say a word, because she knew her cousin had fallen in love with Jean.

They docked in Tampa Florida the following morning, Jessica and her family said their goodbyes as everyone hugged and kissed each other, as they prepared to go back to their normal lives. Jessica's plane back to Dayton was not scheduled to leave until later that night.

"Would you like to go see the Busch Gardens and have dinner while we wait for your flight home?" Jean-Jacques asked her.

"Sure, Jessica said with a smile." They stored her luggage in his car, they went to the Busch Gardens.

They visited the museum in St. Petersburg, they laughed and enjoyed their last day together, until they could meet again. Jean-Jacques drove her to the airport and waved as he watched her plane take off. "*Mwen renmen ou dam mwen.*" He said to her knowing that she would not hear those words.

Jean knew that he would see her soon and he couldn't wait until they meet again. Because he knew that she was meant for him. He smiled as he turned from the big glass window and walked out the airport.

Coming in 2018

His Soulmate

Loving Lexie

Book 1

Coming in 2022

My Jamaican Love

His Soulmate

Loving Lexie

Book 1

Never Should've Loved Him

CHAPTER ONE

Lexie Mitchell was running from her past and a man that she had left behind. Now her past is catching up with her. Lexie left New York under the witness protection program, after she gave information on her husband and his drug ring, and the three murders that he committed. She had testified under oath in a closed hearing against her husband Carlos Garrett. Lexie had to give up her whole life and everything in it.

She was ok with that, because, she had no family really and her husband was a bad person; that if he found her, he would kill her. Lexie was cool with getting a fresh start at life, with a new name and job, in a new city. Now three years later she had finally made new friends and was able to live her life without looking over her shoulder all the time.

She even loved her job as a high school office secretary in Ohio. She even had new hobbies and activities that she loved doing with her friends. Two days a week she would go to Club Majestics and have a few drinks and line dance with her friends, who were always trying to fix her up with someone. Lexie always turned them down, saying that she wasn't looking for a new man in her life right now. Walking into Club Majestics she looked around to see if she could see her friends and that fine looking white guy that always seems to come on the days they were there. She liked seeing him there, knowing he was there always made her feel safe for some reason. Even though he has never said more than hi to her he still made her feel safe when he was in the club. But lately she was having a strange feeling that she was being watched. She shuddered with fear as her mind went back to that day three years ago, and the words that Carlos had spoken to her. Those words rang loud and clear in her mind. Lexie's legs began to get weak as she struggled to find a seat. With her face in her hands, Lexie began to fear for her Life again. Lexie could remember the last time she saw Carlos; it was the night she said she wanted a divorce. And she thought she was gonna die.

Carlos had come home late again after he was out with another woman. She was in the bed waiting up for him again; she was tired of his mess and she was gonna let him know tonight.

"You must think that it's alright for you to stay out all night? You must really think I'm gonna keep sitting around here, waiting for you to come home, while you're out sticking your dick in every bitch that opens her legs." Tandy screamed as she got out of bed and walked to meet Carlos at the door. He smelled like some women's cheap perfume, and sex.

Tandy saw burgundy lipstick on the collar of his white shirt. Tandy wanted to slap the shit out of him, but she knew that he would beat the crap out of her like a man. He tried to go around her, but she got all grabbed her by the arms, "take your ass back to sleep if you know what's best for you Tandy." He said as he moved her out of the way and went towards the restroom to take a shower.

"Carlos, I want a divorce" Tandy said softly. This was the hardest decision, Tandy had to make.

"Ha ha," Carlos laughed in Tandy's face and continued on to the restroom. He looked over his shoulder and said, "until death do us part remember, babe, so take your pretty little self-back to sleep." At that moment she knew that she had to get away from him, she got up in his face so that he couldn't get past. Carlos he was not gonna let her go on her own, he would kill her first.

Never Should've Loved Him

My Jamaican Love

Never Should've Loved Him

Chapter 1

Sophia Johnson sat at her kitchen nook drinking a cup of tea and looking out her bay window as the sun came up before going into work. She appreciated these times when she could reflect on her life and all that she has been through to get where she is today. So tired of the dating scene, and the lack thereof, there just weren't any men with ambitions, dreams, or family ties anymore.

Walking down the hall to get ready for work, she stopped and looked in the mirror, she stared at herself and wondered why it was so hard to find a man to love her.

I know I'm not the most beautiful woman on earth, but you would think that with my college degree in business and being a business owner, and not one who runs the street, but one who has a good head on her shoulders; that someone would think I was worth taking a second look at. Oh well, no need to dwell on it now, there is work to be done, and feeling sorry for myself is not gonna make it any better.

Walking to her room she got dressed for work, pulling her long straight black hair into a ponytail that hung down the middle of her back, putting on some shimmering lip gloss and her favorite perfume. Looking in the mirror one last time she winked at herself and walked out of the room towards the front of the house for her car keys.

Leaving the house on her way to work Sophia let her mind wonder what it would be like to have someone to come home to at the end of the day, someone to hug her when she had a long day at work. Someone that she could ask how their day went, someone to have her back and all that good stuff, Someone to share their life with and start a family with.

Driving through the light Sophia took pride in the fact that she is the owner of 'Sophia's Gourmet Bakery' that supplies baked goods to restaurants big and small, as well as the neighborhood and small businesses.

Her friends and family were proud of the accomplishments that she has made, especially after getting through a bad relationship and being left at the altar by her fiancé. And finding out that he was living a double life Sophia has put her life back together and back on track, taking time out to get to know herself all over again on her own terms. And finally found out what she really wants and needs in her life; now that she is stable and confident enough to take on new adventures and relationships. She's ready to get back out there and find Mr. Right, but is he even out there?

Sophie pulled up into her parking space at her shop and sat in the car and just took it all in, this was her pride and joy, getting out and opening up the shop for the day her assistant Sidney was already there taking care of things. She was glad that she hired her, she thought with a smile as she looked around and saw that she had filled up all the display cases with cakes, brownies, pies and more for the day. She has even started making a batch of her favorite raspberry truffles. Every day they make something different to place on the counter for customers to enjoy when they come in. Her morning was going smoothly, and her shop was full of customers.

Kayla Jones walked into 'Sophia's Gourmet Treats', at twelve-thirty, to see if her friend is free for lunch like she does every day at the same time.

"Hey, Sophie, girl how's your day going? Are you free for lunch?"

"Kay, girl what's up? Yes, I'm free, give me a few minutes to let Sidney know that I'm going to lunch." As Kayla and Sophia walked out of the bakery headed to lunch, Sophia noticed a blue BMW pulling into her parking lot, she could not see who the driver was because it had tinted windows.

"I called Karman, to join us for lunch," Kayla said.

"Oh great, this is what I needed a girls' lunch with my two best friends," Sophia said happily.

Sitting in the Italian restaurant, with her girls, Sophia enjoyed an Italian chicken and pasta dish with steamed vegetables on the side and some buttery bread. While Kayla had her all-time favorite crusted chicken with penne noodles and their homemade creamy alfredo sauce and a side salad, and Karman had a tour of Italy with veggie lasagna, crusted chicken parmesan, and garlic spaghetti with a side salad also. And as always, they talked about men, finding a man for Sophia.

"Sophia, I have someone I want you to meet" Karman said.

"His name is Josh Wendell. I told him about you a couple of weeks ago, and he wants to take you out for drinks."

Shaking her head Sophia said, "you guys know that I don't like blind dates."

"This is not a blind date Sophie, this is just drinks or something, girl. Get out and enjoy yourself for a change, all you do is work, work, and more work." Kay said.

"And besides how do you expect to meet Mr. right if you don't get out and socialize sometimes," Karman commented.

"Yeah, you need to get out." Kayla said with a smile on her face. Even though her friends were having a conversation about her and her dating life all during lunch she still enjoyed lunch and being with her girls.

She just hated going on blind dates; they never seem to work out. But I'm not gonna dwell on it today or any day. I will just enjoy my lunch and my girls.

Back at the shop, Sophia went over the midday totals with Sidney. Sophia got all her paperwork done before closing for the day. She ordered supplies for the following month and was about to start closing down the bakery when she looked out the big picture window at the front of her shop and noticed the blue BMW again in the parking lot.

Hmm, maybe it belongs to someone visiting the other shops in the area. She thought to herself. Straightening up the shop before leaving, Sophia checked to see if the car was still there, and it was no longer there. Now that is just weird the car was just there thirty minutes ago, she thought to herself. Oh, well she thought.

ABOUT THE AUTHOR

I am a mother of two boys and a girl. I'm the oldest of my four siblings. I have two grandchildren who I love dearly. I am the oldest of a brother and three sisters I grew up in Dayton Ohio, I got to do a little traveling as a kid my father was in the service.

Some of my hobbies include cooking, baking, reading, and spending time with my family and friends. I have always had a passion for books, my first real paying job was Madden Hills Library, I could sit and read books for hours at a time and recall everything that I read from any book.

If you would like to email Nadine for more about her new titles or leave comments about her books please feel free to at nadine.hanley16@gmail.com or njsbooks16@yahoo.com She would love to hear from you.

Thanks

Much Love

Nadine

Never Should've Loved Him

Never Should've Loved Him